CONSTABLE ON THE COAST

Further adventures in the series which inspired TV's Heartbeat.

From time to time Constable Nick must leave his beat at Aidensfield to assist his colleagues, and at the height of the holiday season he finds himself in the popular seaside resort of Strensford. He investigates a message in a bottle which suggests a girl is being held hostage, then finds himself helping a film crew. Why would a family of children ride donkeys at dawn – while facing backwards? Why would a lone woman stand on the cliffs and gaze out to sea for two hours every day? These and a host of other problems generate new constabulary duties for Nick!

CONSTABLE ON THE COAST

CONSTABLE ON THE COAST

by

Nicholas Rhea

Magna Large Print Books
Long Preston, North Yorkshire,
BD23 4ND, England.

British Library Cataloguing in Publication Data.

Rhea, Nicholas
   Constable on the coast.

   A catalogue record of this book is
   available from the British Library

   ISBN   978-0-7505-2794-1

First published in Great Britain in 2006 by Robert Hale Ltd.

Cover illustration © Barbara Walker by arrangement with
Robert Hale Ltd.

Published in Large Print 2007 by arrangement with
Robert Hale Limited

X000 000 027 6368

Magna Large Print is an imprint of Library Magna Books Ltd.

Printed and bound in Great Britain by
T.J. (International) Ltd., Cornwall, PL28 8RW

AUTHOR'S NOTE

The Yorkshire coastline begins at the mouth of the River Tees near Middlesbrough and stretches south around some of England's most spectacular scenery to terminate near the mouth of the River Humber. That point is several miles to the south-east of Kingston-upon-Hull. The precise length is debatable due to countless bays and nabs, but it is in the region of a hundred miles (c. 185 km).

During my time as the village constable of Aidensfield, roughly half that coastline lay within the North Riding of Yorkshire, while the other half was in the East Riding. The approximate halfway mark was the East Riding's Filey with its famous Brigg.

The entire stretch includes some of England finest resorts such as Whitby, Scarborough (the Queen of Watering Places and England's first spa resort), Filey, Bridlington and Hornsea, along with intriguing smaller seaside communities like Staithes, Robin Hood's Bay and Withernsea. Between Filey and Flamborough Head lie Bempton Cliffs, England's largest mainland breeding ground for gannets, puffins, razorbills, kittiwakes and guillemots. The public can walk along Bempton Cliffs to observe the birds below, an unforgettable experience in the nesting season.

There are splendid sandy beaches and rocky coves the entire length of the coast which is renowned for its stirring tales of fisherfolk, smugglers and brave lifeboat men. Lighthouses continue to stand like lonely sentinels to guard the shoreline and warn ships of danger.

Smaller boats make use of the busy harbours while larger vessels such as tankers can be seen on the horizon, moving steadily through the swell of the waves.

On shore, though, there is evidence of a very ancient history dating to the period before man walked the earth, with fossils and skeletons of dinosaurs being found, and there are more modern reminders in the form of Whitby's ruined abbey, Scarborough's magnificent castle and Bridlington's priory church. These famous sights exist alongside centuries of tradition and a way of life which has changed little down the years.

Not surprisingly, there is much to do and see along this coastline. Even if these communities fascinate their visitors, they are all working towns and villages, with some retaining their fishing vessels while others have come to rely heavily on tourism. Holiday-makers and day-trippers swarm to these places in their hundreds and thousands, bringing a non-stop series of problems such as losing their wallets or purses, getting drunk or lost or both, breaking bones, being swept out to sea in dinghies, dropping dead in the street, falling down cliffs or even getting drowned either by accident or design. They crash their cars, overturn their caravans, set the moors or forests on fire and forget where they have parked their cars, or from where their bus leaves for home. In short, tourists in large groups are little more than problem-producing people for whom there should be a congestion charge. Although individually, tourists are usually charming and quite wonderful. Of course, we are all tourists at some stage of our lives, probably never thinking that our actions can sometimes ruin or damage the scenery we so love and enjoy.

Many of the less adventurous return to

their favourite haunt year after year even if the weather can be chilly with cold winds known as 'nor'-easters' and thick fogs known as roaks or sea-frets. Because of the seasonal influx, which used to begin at Easter and continue until mid-September after the school holidays ended, the coastal population swelled far beyond the usual residential numbers. Today, the visitor season continues throughout the year, but in both instances the work of the local constabulary is correspondingly increased. Much of this extra work arises through the stupidity of some visitors while the daft and infantile behaviour of certain adults has to be experienced to be believed. It is often said that the work of the police and other emergency services is to clear up the mess left behind by the great British public – that is especially the case in our seaside resorts. To cope with such problems over lengthy periods, there used to exist a mutual aid scheme whereby the coastal police divisions could seek assistance from their inland colleagues who were not swamped to the same extent. Just as mutual aid schemes existed for matters like industrial unrest, race meetings, top football matches, major incidents and other large-scale events, so a similar scheme had been devised to cope with sea-side tourists during the peak of the season.

It happened that my time at Aidensfield coincided with a sharp increase in the ownership of family cars. Instead of relying on trains and buses to carry visitors to the seaside, usually for a week or perhaps a fortnight to make the trip worthwhile, families changed their behaviour and went by car instead but things changed even more because they only stayed for the day.

That was preferable to, and cheaper than, spending a week or a fortnight in one of those infamous seaside boarding houses. This social change meant the day-tripper was born; it became a new phenomenon which suddenly made off-street car parks very necessary. Without somewhere to put all those incoming vehicles, the narrow streets of our coastal communities would be blocked within a very short time and commerce would suffer. Consequently this social change urgently demanded some kind of control over the incomers as they flooded into the resorts at peak periods.

By directing them all to car parks, a mini-mum of control was exercised. The trouble was that visitors all tended to arrive around the same time and so swamp the unfortunate traffic duty constables as the incomers all sought a parking place as close as possible to the beach, the toilets, an ice-cream chalet and a fish-and-chip shop. This kind of problem was generated if, say, one family decided they were going to have a very early start to beat the crowds and get a good parking space. What such people did not realize was that an identical thought was present at precisely the same moment in thousands of other people. In other words, everyone set off early to beat the rush, only to arrive together in a slow-moving crocodile of cars all seeking the same parking space.

The result was they drove round and round for hours trying to find a space – even in the heady days of the 1960s, this created traffic congestion and caused tempers to fray.

From time to time, therefore, I found myself drafted temporarily into Strensford, Whitby or Scarborough to help the local bobbies cope with that rush of hot-blooded seaside visitors, all of whom were determined to have a good time whatever the cost in sweat and anxiety. Sometimes I would have to live in lodgings and spend a week or even longer plodding the seaside beat, both by day and by night, and sometimes I would be sent across the moors to spend just a single day at one or other of the resorts. A day in Staithes or Robin Hood's Bay, for example, could be positively marvellous and some of my earlier coastal adventures are featured in *Constable by the Sea* published by Robert Hale in 1985 and now out of print.

That collection of yarns features a long period of duty in Strensford but in this volume I shall relate events which happened from time to time during shorter visits.

NICHOLAS RHEA

CHAPTER 1

One of the cliff-top vantage points to the north of Strensford commands views in all directions. When standing on the 450-foot high promontory, called Strensford Ness, it is possible to look east and west along sheer rocky cliff-faces which seem to stretch into infinity, while to the north is the endlessly moving grey of the sea and behind, to the south, the distant bulk of the North York Moors.

That vantage point, so popular with hikers and visitors, is both dramatic and beautiful, but it is also windswept to such an extent that it is positively dangerous at times. A person standing near the cliff edge would have no chance in a powerful gale – they could be swept over to crash hundreds of feet onto the rocks below, perhaps never to be found. Here, the tide roars in to cover the rocks with thumping, foaming water and such is the power of the waves that they would smash anyone and anything careless enough to linger among those rocks. Not for nothing is this part of the coastline known as the Devil's Graveyard. Even in a moderately severe storm, wooden sailing vessels have been smashed to matchwood in a matter of days and on those occasions when human bodies are known to have been lying among the rocks – suicides perhaps, or casualties swept in from seawrecks – they have been carried away on the first reasonably normal high tide with never a bone remaining. Their ultimate fate was always unknown.

In examining this cliff, the suspicious mind of a police officer would always ask this question if a body was found below: did he fall or was he pushed?

At low tide, there is no discernible beach below this headland. As the water recedes, so it uncovers yet more boulders and rock-pools, all slippery with deep, slimy layers of seaweed and inaccessible from above. There is no footpath along this part of the shore and although past stories of smugglers are told about this area, no evidence of their activities has survived. There are no hand-carved steps from sea level to the top of the cliff; no evident mooring for a boat, no sign of a landing stage, no form of accessible shelter or harbour of any kind. If there had been smugglers here in the past, they must have been very daring and determined to come ashore at this point, but of course, since then, the coastline has been drastically altered by the constant pounding of heavy seas. Any kind of haven must have been swept to destruction long, long ago.

Access to the headland itself by the public is possible and indeed a public footpath skirts the edge of the cliff. There are warning signs to say the cliff is unstable at specified points, consequently the path weaves about like a snake so that in places sections of it are a considerable distance inland. Notices advising the public not to venture too close are positioned near the most dangerous places. There are no railings or fencing, it being considered too risky to attempt to erect them – the mere act of hammering posts into the ground could dislodge a considerable amount of the cliff and carry any workers with it. Common sense from the rambling public is hoped for but not always offered. It must be said that local people seldom venture anywhere near the edge, although some visitors do risk life and limb by trying to peer down to the sea directly below.

It has never been known how many people have lost their lives through getting too close to the edge – if they were from afar and alone, and if they fell either to their deaths or suffered dreadful injuries, it is highly likely no one would know their fate. Even if they survived the fall, the sea would soon finish them off and their bodily remains would be swept away at the very next high tide, and lost for ever. They might be listed as missing persons, but the true reason for their disappearance would never be known.

Clearly, Strensford Ness was the ideal place to commit suicide – or murder. If someone fell over accidentally and landed on the rocks at the base, then of course the emergency services – fire, police, ambulance, RAF rescue and coastguards – would all be alerted by anyone witnessing the incident, but successful recovery of the injured party or their remains always depended upon the time of the next high tide.

During my occasional sorties to Strensford whilst on duty, I tried to visit the Ness, not only for the splendour of the view but also to look down from on high to check whether the base of the cliff offered anything of interest, either professional or personal: dead bodies, wreckage, the discarded evidence of a crime, large items of litter or even bottles containing messages from far-off places. Not that a glass bottle would survive for long among those rocks and seas.

An added factor was that I could not have personally recovered any such thing, but at least I could alert the necessary authorities if my discovery, whatever it was, was sufficiently serious and accessible, such as a human body or discarded safe!

It was during one of those periodic visits on a Saturday afternoon that I noticed a lone woman standing some forty or fifty yards inland from the tip of the Ness. She was the only person in sight. It was a bright and sunny August day with a brisk breeze coming off the sea and fetching with it the distinctive scents of salt and seaweed; at times, the breeze brought in small clouds of sea-spray after a large wave had crashed against the base of the cliff or dispersed over the rocks below. And, of course, there was the ever-present sound of the restless sea, crashing waves and cries of herring gulls soaring and gliding on the air currents. I was not unduly surprised to see someone else walking alone – many people came this way if they wanted to escape the crowds and have a short, quiet time to commune with nature. It was a popular destination for people who wanted to be alone.

As I walked along the winding path,

clearly visible in my police uniform, I was looking out for anything which might have been of professional interest to me. This walk was a pleasant diversion from our regular patrols, and I never tired of plodding along this very scenic part of one of the town's more remote beats. As a matter of record, this distant part of Strensford was not patrolled every day but the town inspector felt that, once in a while, by day and by night at irregular intervals, there should be a visible police presence.

That was my role on this occasion and, before returning to more mundane tasks, I just had time to walk to the tip of the Ness and check whether anyone had fallen or jumped off, or whether anyone had disposed of stolen goods by throwing them off the cliff.

Not that I could do much about any of those matters, except to record them, or identify, with binoculars, any possible stolen goods or relics of them which might have been discarded here. It was amazing where thieves disposed of stolen but emptied safes!

As I walked along the well-designated path, the woman remained motionless, standing with her hands clasped before her body as the breeze ruffled her grey hair. A slightly built woman little more than five feet tall, she was dressed in a green-checked skirt, a white blouse and a green cardigan and I guessed she would be in her early fifties. As my slow pace carried me forward, I did not like to stare but could see she was apparently gazing out to sea, almost as if she was expecting someone to appear on the horizon. Did she have a husband or son on board one of those ships which were always passing along the coast? Was she looking for some kind of signal from a passing ship? A flashing light perhaps or toot of a horn. Or was she a birdwatcher, hoping to catch sight of some rare visitor to our shores? She was too far away to speak to and I did not wish to intrude upon her solitude. Besides, the reason for her presence was none of my business.

I reached the extent of my patrol, looked down into the abyss beneath the Ness where the angry sea boiled over the rocks and sent spray high into the air as the mighty waves beat the cliff with roars and slaps, and saw nothing of interest. When I returned the way I had come, the woman was still there, motionless in her place of observation, and she did not acknowledge my presence.

I glanced in her direction, an act which I

hoped would inform her that I was aware of her even if I did not wish to approach her or be a nuisance, and then I walked on. If she had wanted assistance of any kind, then I felt I had made myself available – she could have hailed me. She was still standing there when I left the area to resume a more normal patrol of the town's northern environs. The incident itself was so minor and innocuous that it was not worth recording in my official notebook and as I continued to supervise the rest of my beat, the matter was relegated to the back of my mind.

I thought no more about it until the following Tuesday afternoon. Once again I was performing further seaside duties in Strensford and found myself patrolling along the cliffs towards the Ness. It was another fine and bright August afternoon with a stiff wind off the sea but with clear blue skies and, like the previous Saturday, there was no one else on the cliff walk other than myself. But when I crested the final rise, I realized the woman was again standing in the same place, gazing steadfastly out to sea. She was dressed in the same clothes as she had worn on Saturday and, as before, she totally ignored my presence.

I continued about my patrol, peeped over

the cliff to see the tide was right in and at its highest point with monstrous waves beating the cliffs thanks to the power of the wind coming off the sea. The shape of the cliffs amplified the sounds but I could see nothing down there except the whiteness of the breaking waves; no rocks were visible and if there had been anything of interest, it would have been swept away long before my arrival.

An hour later, when I had resumed my patrol, the town sergeant came to visit me at one of my conference points. He was Sergeant Morris who had been at Strensford for most of his service and who was heading for retirement within the year. He was a large bear of a man with white hair, a rather crumpled appearance and very slow movements; no one had ever seen him flustered or angry and, because he had been stationed here so long, he was virtually part of the Strensford scenery.

'All correct, Sergeant,' I said, as he ambled to my side in his rolling gait.

'Out here, you'd wonder where everyone has got to.' He smiled. 'I can tell you, though, the town centre's like a honey pot. People, cars, kids and ice creams everywhere. You're far better out here, Nick, it's more like your own part of the world. Nice and quiet.'

'There wasn't a soul on the Ness,' I said. 'I would have thought holidaymakers would want to go out there for a walk, if only for the view!'

'It depends on the holidaymakers.' He smiled. 'There's those who go for ice creams, fish and chips, kiss-me-quick hats and amusement arcades, and others who come at weekends for a bit of bracing fresh air in a peaceful place. It's the latter you'll find out at Ness, but probably not during the school holidays. They turn August over to the kids and their families, it's them who's packing the town centre and beach areas right now. They won't find their way out to Ness.'

'Thanks, now I understand,' I said, thinking of my own children also on holiday. We were due to head for a rented cottage in the Lake District in a few days' time. My children loved the lakes, preferring them to the seashore.

Then I remembered the lone woman. 'Ah, but Sergeant, there was a woman on the Ness. Just standing there. She was there on Saturday afternoon as well. I just wondered who she is, whether she's all right or in need of help.'

'She's there every afternoon, Nick. And I mean every afternoon, seven days a week,

January through to December. She stands there for a couple of hours, from two until four, gazing out to sea. She's there in all weathers, snow, hail, wind, fog, rain, sunshine. Never fails to appear.'

'Why?'

'No one knows. It's just something she does. Some people go and fly kites, others walk dogs or look for rare flowers. She goes and stands on the Ness.'

'Who is she?'

'Her name is Eunice. Eunice Napier. Miss Napier. She lives in a flat in Church Square, one of those big Victorian houses with cellars like ballrooms and bedrooms with fireplaces big enough and smart enough to live in. The whole house is let as flats. She's never had a job that I am aware of, so she must have a private income of some sort. I think she might own the entire building where she lives, renting off the other space as her income. There's half a dozen flats in there. She has no family that I know about – but apart from that, no one knows much about her, except that every afternoon she walks along to the Ness and stands looking out to sea. She's quite sane, if that's what's worrying you, she's not likely to jump off the cliff.'

'So how long has she been doing that?'

'No one knows for certain. I've lived here almost all my life and I think she started before the war. I can't ever remember her not doing that. In fact, the local people who know her just accept it as normal now. No one bothers to ask why.'

'There must be a reason,' I said, almost under my breath.

'I'm sure there must, but it's nothing to do with us, Nick. It's her life, she's not breaking any law or being a public nuisance. She simply goes out there for two hours and then goes home. If she was an artist or a photographer doing her stuff or just walking a dog, no one would bat an eyelid, but because she just stands there and never says a word to anybody, people get puzzled.'

'Like me!'

'Exactly. So just accept her as one of the sights of Strensford. Now, we've been getting reports of visitors' parked cars obstructing Blake Street, so let's go and see if there's any truth in it, and if so, whether we can sort it out.'

And so I returned to normal policing.

For the rest of that summer, I travelled across the moors to Strensford on several occasions, usually to undertake a single day's duty before returning home in the evening. On one or two occasions, I found myself returning to the Ness during routine patrols, and if I happened to be there between two and four in the afternoon, Miss Napier was always standing on her spot, looking out to sea. And she never spoke or acknowledged me in any way, neither did I attempt to strike up a conversation.

However, although I accepted that her routine had absolutely nothing to do with me and that it should not concern me in the slightest way, plus the fact I should mind my own business, I couldn't avoid being intrigued by her behaviour. I could not do anything about it, of course, but over the weeks I could not ignore the niggling feeling that there must be a perfectly logical reason for her unusual practice of standing alone on the Ness for two hours in all weathers.

Then a curious coincidence happened. I had to deal with the sudden death of an elderly gentleman in Strensford, the reason being that I was called to the scene when he collapsed in the street. He died very soon afterwards in hospital but no one knew his name and so I was charged with the task of establishing his identity. He carried no form of identity, although there was a housekey in his trousers pocket. It looked like a back-door key, not a Yale of the kind borne by many front doors.

When I began to ask from shops and houses in and around the street where he had collapsed, I was directed to a tiny cottage in an alley. My informants had said it was owned by an elderly man called Henley who appeared to match the description of the casualty, and when I knocked on the door, the place was clearly deserted. I rang the bell of the neighbouring door and a lady answered. When I described the incident with a brief description of the gentleman concerned, she said, 'Oh dear, it does sound like Mr Henley.'

'Would you be prepared to come to the hospital and look at him to see whether it is him?' I asked.

Although the idea of looking at a dead neighbour's face did not appeal very much, she bravely agreed to help and so we established that the dead man did live at the little cottage – No. 5 Lilac Yard – and that his name was Joseph Henley, a widower in his early eighties.

There would he a post mortem to establish the cause of death, and I made sure the coroner was informed, but in the meantime I had to try and trace any of his relatives so that I could notify them of his death. The only way to do that was to search his house in the hope I might find an address book or some other records, or even his will. Performing that kind of search was not particularly pleasant because it felt like an invasion of privacy but in cases like this it was necessary. Indeed, sometimes we discovered valuables which required protection from thieves and burglars who might have taken advantage of a person's death to raid his property. Even in the 1960s, such callous rogues were around. Valuables might consist of jewellery, antiques or personal treasures, but often in the case of elderly people, it was cash which they had concealed in all manner of unlikely places. In searching for mundane things like address books or diaries, we often turned up hoards of money and our task was to safeguard that kind of personal property by removing it to the police station or perhaps to the deceased's bank or solicitor.

And so I prepared to search Mr Henley's cottage.

The key which had been in his pocket fitted the back door and so I started in the tiny and rather sparsely appointed kitchen, the most obvious place to keep personal items.

That was because many people conducted their domestic administration on the kitchen table, dealing with matters such as writing letters and keeping household records. Bills were kept in tea caddies, spare cash was in jam jars and correspondence was often stuffed into kitchen drawers. As I began my quest, I found domestic papers such as rate demands, electricity accounts, gas bills and so forth, but nothing bearing the name and address of anyone who might be a relative or friend. There was no Christmas card list, for example, and no list of childrens' or relatives' birthdays or their addresses. From those initial searches, it seemed that Mr Henley had lived a very lonely life, although I did not forget that he was a widower. Surely his late wife must have had friends and relatives? And lists containing their names and addresses? I found no papers in his tiny lounge, not even a newspaper or magazine although there was a small TV set and a radio. I hunted under the cushions of his chair without finding anything, and likewise a search of the pantry, paying due attention to things like the bread-bin and biscuit tins, produced nothing.

The short, steep, narrow and very dark staircase led into a tiny bathroom with a washbasin and toilet, but there were no personal papers there, and off the landing I noticed two further doors, both closed and both in need of a coat of paint. I opened one – it led into his bedroom, a dingy place with a double bed, a wardrobe and dressing table but little else. The bedcovers were in place, if not arranged very carefully, but there were no pictures on the walls, the curtains were thin and dirty, and the floor was covered with linoleum with a clip mat at the side of his bed. There was a bedside table bearing a lamp and a library edition of a cowboy novel.

I searched in all the usual places – under the mattress, under the bed, in the drawers and wardrobe (both under it and on top of it) and even in the pockets of his best suit, his only suit in fact. I looked under the clip mat and opened an ancient suitcase. There was nothing. And then I turned my attention to the second landing door to find myself in the smallest of rooms with the thin curtains closed and an air of decay about it. I opened the curtains because I needed more light. There was no bed but standing under the window was a small card-table covered in green baize with a dining-style chair tucked beneath it. There was a single wardrobe against a wall but all around on the floor were papers – old newspapers or magazines by the look of it, all packed neatly into cardboard boxes. And there were several on the table, each open but lying on top of those beneath, and the top one was opened at the births, deaths and marriages column of the *Strensford Gazette*. It was smothered in layers of dust and I guessed it had not been touched for years.

I went across to read the entries and, under forthcoming marriages, found a reference to a man called Bernard Henley, the son of Joseph and Dorothy Henley. The date of the paper was 20 September, 1938, and the announcement said, 'The engagement is announced between Bernard, the only son of Joseph and Dorothy Henley of Strensford, and Eunice, the only daughter of Paul and Irene Napier also of Strensford.' So there was a son! I knew that Mr Henley was a widower so where did I begin to search for his son? If his engagement was announced in 1938, I guessed that under normal circumstances he would be around twenty-one or so which meant he would have been born around 1918, give or take a year or two either way.

At the time of my research, that would put his age at around fifty – and that was compatible with the apparent age of the deceased Mr Henley, who looked as if he was in his late seventies. So if Bernard was fifty or thereabouts, where was he? And why was this announcement laid out in this manner, smothered in the dust of decades?

It was then that the significance of what I was reading struck home.

Eunice Napier! The woman I'd seen standing on Strensford Ness and gazing out to sea. So if Bernard had been engaged to her, what had gone wrong? And where was he? I couldn't leave immediately to go looking for Eunice because I had yet to find any official papers, such as his birth certificate. I started by looking through the other papers on the table, all copies of the *Strensford Gazette*, and found that those beneath the engagement announcement had been left open at reports of football and cricket matches. As I scanned them, it was quickly evident that the name of Bernard Henley was very prominent – clearly, he was an outstanding sportsman who excelled at both football and cricket. I discovered the same when I looked briefly at other papers packed into boxes. They had been stuffed into the cardboard boxes in date sequence, but left open at pages which mentioned Bernard's name. Clearly, Mr Henley had been immensely proud of his son – or was it Mrs Henley who had been so proud? I would never know.

My search was incomplete however because I needed to find proof of his birth and it was not until I opened the wardrobe that I found another cardboard box containing the more personal stuff.

There I found a birth certificate in Joseph Henley's name, his wedding certificate and other things like family photos, some clearly depicting Joseph, his wife and young son. In spite of hunting assiduously, however, I did not find a will nor any sign of a bank account or solicitor who might act for him, nor was there any address for Bernard except for the previous family home. Before moving to his tiny cottage, it was evident Joseph, Dorothy and Bernard had lived at no. 42, Beech Street in Strensford, and after Dorothy had died, he had sold that house to move into something smaller and more manageable. There was no hint of Bernard being involved in that move and it did not explain Bernard's disappearance. No. 42, Beech Street was the last address I had for him and so I decided I should call there, just to be sure he wasn't living there! After all, he might have fallen out with his family.

Satisfied that I had completed a competent

search, I returned to the police station with the necessary personal documents which would be included in the file of his death but I was acutely aware that I had not traced a solitary relative. So who would take charge of the funeral arrangements? Deal with the legal side of things? Dispose of the house? I felt sure the coroner would have access to the legal systems and procedures which were available to deal with this kind of problem. Before I sat down to compile the official account of my search for Joseph's family, I knew I must contact Eunice Napier. She was the only person who may be able to throw some light on the whereabouts of Bernard Henley. Sergeant Morris was on duty and so I found him in the Sergeants' Office and asked if he knew Eunice's home address.

He had said she lived in a flat in Church Square but hadn't given me the number and when he asked the reason for my query, he nodded his pleasure at this outcome.

'Well done, Nick,' he said, giving me her flat number. 'I can't answer your question so you'll have to talk to her. She'll be home now, from her vigil on the Ness.'

On the way, I called at the Henleys' former home but the current occupants had no idea who the Henleys were and had never been in contact with them; they'd only been at that address for a couple of years. So I continued to flat 4 at No. 6, Church Square. The house was in a terrace of large Victorian houses, all brick built. I walked into the communal front door and went up the stairs, following the signs to flats 2, 3 and 4. Flat 4 was at the very top, probably where it was quiet although it would have splendid views across the cliffs and sea. If Miss Napier was owner of the house, she would he able to pick and choose her own home. I found myself outside a smart and very solid green door with brass fittings and a brass bell-push on the door-jamb. I pressed it and heard it ring inside.

I heard her coming to the door but before opening it, she called, 'Who is it?'

'It's PC Rhea from the police station,' I said, not wishing to confuse her by announcing I was from Aidensfield. 'I wonder if you can spare me a minute?'

'Oh dear, the police, yes of course,' and I heard her unlock the door and withdraw a couple of bolts. Then the door opened.

At close quarters, I could see she was a tall, very slender and elegant lady dressed in silky clothes. Her hair was grey in keeping with her age, which I estimated to be around fifty, and she wore a pair of rimless spectacles over which she gazed at me with evident curiosity.

'Good heavens, what have I done?' and she smiled a warm welcome. 'I do hope it is nothing serious. But forgive me, you must come in. Can I get you a cup of tea? The kettle is on. I usually have a cup myself around this time and it would he nice to share it with someone. Do come in and sit down.'

She led me into the lounge, a huge room with a beautiful fireplace containing a welcoming fire, and bade me sit on the leather sofa while she busied herself with my tea. At this point, she did not ask the reason for my presence but vanished into the kitchen where I could hear the sound of tea cups, saucers and a kettle on the boil. I looked around the room, admiring the expensive furniture, the shelves full of books, the cupboard full of ceramics, the grandfather clock, the thick carpet and heavy wallpaper. It was the home of a person with both money and style. Then she returned with a tray which she placed on a coffee table, and then settled in one of the armchairs.

'Now,' she said. 'This is intriguing. While it is mashing, why don't you tell me what brings you here?'

'It is quite a delicate matter,' I started, not entirely sure how she would react to my questions. 'I might add I have seen you on the Ness...'

'Ah, that young constable! I saw you the other day. It's not often we get policemen patrolling up there. I go there a lot.'

'I'm not from Strensford,' I told her, stressing my name again and explaining the reason for my temporary presence in the town before adding, 'I learned of your name from the sergeant, Sergeant Morris. He told me who you were.'

'Ah yes, a nice man, an ideal policeman for this kind of small town.'

At this, she decided it was time to pour the tea and so I paused in my chatter as she provided me with a cup with milk, offering me sugar which I declined, and then proffering a plate of chocolate biscuits. I took one.

'So how can I help you, PC Rhea?'

'I don't want you to think I am prying into your private life,' I began. 'But an elderly gentleman died in town earlier today. He collapsed in the street. His name is Joseph Henley.'

'Oh dear, poor Joseph,' was all she said, even though her face showed immediate signs of sorrow. 'How dreadful! I had no idea. So how did it happen?'

I explained, then added, 'I am dealing with the sudden death enquiry and when I was searching his house, trying to establish whether he had any relatives or where they lived, I found a newspaper containing an announcement of an engagement. Bernard, who I presume is his son, was engaged to Eunice Napier, which I think is you.'

'Really? You found that? Yes, it is me. And you mean he had kept that paper, after all this time?'

'Yes, along with lots of others, many dealing with Bernard's sporting achievements. All kept in boxes in a small bedroom.'

'I had no idea, even though I popped in regularly. We would sit in his little lounge and chat and sometimes I would make him a meal, or invite him here. We got on well; he was a lovely man. He had no one, you know. No one at all. But how sad to die like that ... all alone. So how can I help you, PC Rhea?'

'I wanted to confirm that you were the girl Bernard was engaged to, and I had hoped you might tell me where to find him, so that I can tell him about his father.'

'Yes, I am Bernard's fiancée,' and I noticed a further sadness appear on her face. 'We were going to get married.'

'Were going to?'

'Bernard disappeared, PC Rhea. During the war. He was called up by the RAF. He became a fighter pilot and was later declared missing in action. MIA. He disappeared on a mission and has never been seen since. His body has never been found so no one knows whether he is alive or not. I live in hope, all the time. And so did Mr Henley.'

'I'm sorry.'

'Bernard had so much promise; he was such a nice man. His parents were devastated and so was I. Bernard and I used to meet on the Ness, where you saw me. We'd go for walks and he always said that one day, when he had made a lot of money, we would travel the world. He would point out to sea, from where you saw me, saying that was the gateway to the world. Across the sea, he said, there were riches and adventures beyond our dreams ... and so I go there now, to look and remember, and to try and wonder what it might have been like. I have never been overseas, you see, not once, and I never had another boyfriend because I've always thought Bernard would return one day. And I still do. I am still waiting, PC Rhea. Do you think I am a silly romantic old woman?'

'No,' I said. 'I don't. I admire you for your

fortitude and belief. I came to see you because I thought you might be able to put me in touch with some of Joseph's family, I need to tell them about his death.'

'There is no one,' she said. 'After his wife died, there was just Bernard, wherever he is. I'm probably his family, but of course, I am not related to him. So who will see to things? You know, the funeral and so forth.'

'In cases like this, where there are no relatives, there are legal procedures to deal with the estate and the funeral, and anything else associated with the death.'

'Yes, I know, but I'll arrange the funeral, PC Rhea, and see to the house and his personal effects, it's the least I can do. For Bernard.'

'That would be a great help,' I said. 'I'm dealing with the sudden death report and the coroner, so I'll record your name as our official contact. Thanks for this, it helps a lot.'

'Bernard will he sorry to learn of his father's death, but he will be pleased I am able to help while he's away,' she said.

'Yes, I'm sure he will,' I said, remembering to use the present tense.

If my patrols along the shoreline produced that intriguing story, they also provided another puzzle. I was working an early turn in Strensford which meant starting at 6 a.m. and working until 2 p.m., and part of my patrol was along the cliff top close to the western side of the town. This was the smart side of Strensford with large houses, parks and open spaces rich with flowers in the spring and summer. The domestic premises, comprising mainly large Victorian terrace houses, commanded extensive views across the sea and were not troubled with noisy things like amusement arcades, dodgems, fish-and-chip shops, clubs and pubs. The harbourside and all that went with it was a long way off, nicely out of view and out of earshot. It was a very select part of town which meant there was very little to trouble the police although we did make regular patrols among the houses and streets, if only to show the uniform and keep the residents content in the knowledge that crime was being rigorously prevented in their special part of England.

One of the bonuses for a patrolling constable was to walk along that cliff top on a quiet summer morning before the cars, buses and crowds arrived, and before the ice-cream vans started to ply their trade or the souvenir shops opened to sell buckets, spades and funny hats. It was possible to walk a mile or so along the edge of the cliff, upon a properly surfaced path provided by the council, and from there to gaze down upon the beach from many vantage points. When the tide was out in the early morning, those acres of rich soft sand were marvellous, so smooth and unmarked with visitors' footprints, deckchairs, wind shields and litter.

In the distance, the waves would be ceaselessly moving with their white crests, constantly washing the sand and providing a never-ending sound of moving water. By nine o'clock or shortly afterwards, the first cars would arrive and people would lug their belongings down to the beach via one of the cliff paths. Then the buses with their loads would arrive by coffee time and soon the entire area was buzzing with life, colourful deckchairs and rugs. Only the incoming tide would compel them to leave before going-home time and meant those early morning patrols were something special – I could enjoy the shoreline at its most beautiful and in its natural state as part of my work, a rare privilege.

Others also took advantage of this freedom – early morning swimmers, for example, some of whom took a dip on every day in the year, winter and summer alike; people wanting exercise would run along the beach, sometimes with a dog at their side, and others simply walked beside the waves to get some bracing fresh air before starting their day at work or even at home. I would see kite-fliers, model aircraft enthusiasts, birdwatchers and beachcombers who scoured the high waterline for flotsam or jetsam, or for treasures such as coins and other valuables abandoned by visitors. Some beachcombers made a good income from the things they found on the sands. There may be fishermen too, using long lines which stretched deep into the waves or those digging in the soft sand to seek live bait. Even in the early morning, this kind of activity meant the beach was usually busy but not troublesome for few of these projects were of official concern to the police.

And then one particularly quiet morning, when the tide was far out and the beach almost deserted with not a footprint in the sand, I noticed a curious sight. At first it did not register as being particularly odd because it was nothing more than three small children riding donkeys with a couple of adults walking alongside. One of the adults was a woman, probably the mother of the children, and the other was a grey-haired man. Grandad perhaps? Or the owner of the donkeys? I thought it was the donkeys' owner because I'd seen him around town some mornings, walking his herd of donkeys down to the beach. His red spotted neckerchief was a ready means of identification. Admittedly, it was very early in the morning – a little after 6.30 – and so that was not the time the donkeys began their usual daily stint of taking children for rides. Certainly, visitors would not expect to do that at half-past six on a weekday morning. If only for that reason, the sight was slightly out of the ordinary.

But there was something else peculiar about the sight. It took a few moments for my senses to adjust to the oddity and then I realized the children were sitting with their backs to the donkeys' heads. They were facing the animals' tails as the woman took the reins of one, and the man led the other two. They were walking at a gentle pace, just as seaside donkeys do when working on the sands, and I watched in some puzzlement. Why on earth were the children facing the wrong way? Was it because they were frightened? Or was this their first ride, done in some family manner which would pave the way for future rides? I stood on the cliff top and watched the strange little procession.

When they reached one of the break-waters, the adults led the donkeys around in a circle and started to walk back the way they had come. They were following the first tracks – apart from their footprints, there were no other marks in the virgin sand and as I looked ahead, I saw the tracks began at another breakwater about a hundred yards away. And so the little troupe plodded along to the starting point, turned around and began to retrace their route once more. I wondered how long this odd ritual was going to continue; my own time was limited because I had to make a conference point at a local telephone kiosk in about twenty-five minutes' time so I could spare a few minutes. Those conference points were to enable the office to ring me if I was required to attend to anything, and to make sure I was at a certain place at a certain time in case the sergeant or inspector wanted to pay me a visit. As I watched the troupe plod their way between the breakwaters, I counted six complete circuits before I had to leave. And they were still doing more. By then, the time was heading for seven o'clock and my point was at five minutes past, a few minutes' fast walk away. I realized the children might have to attend school – they appeared to be of school age, even if they were very tiny – but there were no protests from them and no variation in their routine.

And so I was compelled to abandon my vantage point in case my supervisory officers wanted to make contact, but in fact I had no calls at the kiosk, and no visitors during my five minute wait. So I dashed back to the cliff top and was in time to see the procession completing yet another leg of their journey, but this time they returned to the starting point and I saw the children dismount.

The mother gathered them together and walked away after evidently thanking the donkey man for the use of his animals, and he turned around to return along the beach with the donkeys following patiently. For the children, it was almost time for school and for the donkeys, it was almost time for work. I turned away to continue my patrol as the little town was awaking to another day.

In all probability I would have forgotten that incident had my beat not taken me down the pier and along the harbourside. I had two points down there, a means of getting a uniformed bobby to patrol among the seasonal visitors, and as I strolled along with my white gloves in my right hand (we always carried white gloves in those days – ideal for directing traffic in addition to looking quite smart) I saw the red polka-dotted neckerchief of the donkey man. He was weaving through the crowds and I was in time to see him vanish into the gents' toilet. No doubt his little herd of donkeys would wait patiently until his return and I felt sure someone was caring for them. However, the sight of him aroused my interest in the children's reverse riding and I decided to wait until he emerged. From local knowledge, I knew his name was Amos Marshall and he was in his late sixties, a suntanned man with iron grey hair and an easy manner, especially with children and animals. Eventually he emerged and I hailed him. 'Hello, Amos,' I said. 'Can I have a word?'

The look on his face suggested he was terrified I was going to arrest him or tell him I suspected him of some horrible offence; maybe he thought someone had complained about him being cruel to this donkeys, as indeed some holidaymakers were prone to do. So I said, 'You're not in bother, it's just a query.'

'Oh, aye.'

'I saw you this morning taking those

children for rides. Three of them. They were facing the back of the donkeys. I just wondered why.'

'Oh aye. It's for t'measles.'

'Measles?'

'Aye, it's going round t'schools. Yon family allus come for rides when t'measles is about. It stops 'em getting it.'

'How does it stop measles?'

'Dunno, search me. I've no idea. All I know is kids who take those rides never get measles. Never 'ave, not in all my whole life.'

'So why did they face the back of the donkeys?'

'That's what you have to do. Sit 'em facing the back, take 'em nine times around a little course, and then pick three hairs from the donkey's tail and hang 'em round the kids' necks. That'll stop 'em getting t'measles, you can be sure 'o that.'

'So that's what this morning's ritual was all about? Do other families come and do the same thing?'

'No, just them Stokelds, they allus come when measles is about. The family's been doing it for years and years, when my dad and his dad were donkey men, and they pay for the rides. Good for business. And it works.'

I didn't want to detain him longer than necessary because I could see he was anxious to return to his charges, and in any case I did not know what to ask next. I thanked him and let him go.

This smacked of ancient superstition, but who was I to question its effectiveness? If they believed that riding a donkey while facing back-to-front prevented a child from catching measles, I must not cast doubt upon the procedure.

I returned to more mundane matters because a shopkeeper had spotted me and wanted to complain about a parked car which was obstructing the footpath outside his shop.

That was something I could understand.

CHAPTER 2

While some children and indeed adults look for seashells and colourful stones along the tideline and in rock pools, others seek messages in bottles. There is something deeply romantic and almost magical in finding a message contained in a glass bottle which has managed to cross miles of ocean in spite of the dangers, perhaps taking months or even years to do so and perhaps originating in some foreign land. The messages can be in any language, although quite often they are appeals for pen friends written in surprisingly good English. A considerable number which arrive on our north-east coast come from children in Scandinavia, although they have been known to journey to other British shores from France, Spain and Portugal, and even America, Canada and South East Asia. I know of no formal register of such arrivals, nor do I know anything about the confluence of sea currents which is necessary to deposit a bottle on a distant continent after being thrown into the sea thousands of miles away. Is it possible, for example, for a bottle to travel unaided by sea all the way from New Zealand to Scotland? I believe the longest time a bottle has been at sea is 73 years; it was thrown from a ship off Queensland in 1910 and arrived at Moreton Island in 1983.

One popular intention when placing a message in a bottle, and then releasing that bottle upon the sea, is to establish a friendship with a child in another country and if a response is generated, it is through that contact that it is hoped each correspondent will learn something of the other's way of life. There are stories of lifetime friendships and even romances developing from messages in bottles.

I am sure that so long as children play upon our beaches, bottles containing messages will continue to arrive and create immense excitement and interest. It is very rarely however, that such a message is of concern or interest to the police. The usual outcome is that the local newspaper publishes the story and the finder receives a few minutes of fame in response to his or her discovery. What happens afterwards depends almost entirely upon the finder, although the length of time the bottle has been in the water, the content of the message and of course the identity and age of the message's originator, might assist the finder in making a decision. I am sure a lot of such messages are never delivered or never acted upon.

When 12-year-old Jessica Young dis-covered a bottle on the shore at Strensford, therefore, she was understandably excited. It was a Saturday morning in July shortly after nine o'clock and she was enjoying a walk along the beach with her spaniel, Pip. He loved the water and spent most of his time dashing into the smaller waves and running around in sheer exuberance but on this occasion Jessica noticed the bottle bobbing up and down in the deeper waves, a few yards into the sea. She lost no time slipping off her sandals and wading knee-deep into the water, getting the hem of her dress wet whilst doing so, but she managed to grab the bottle before the tide swept it back out to sea and beyond her reach. With her trophy, she hurried back to the higher part of the beach as Pip continued to splash and enjoy the water. She examined it before trying to open it and saw it was one of Hicksons' clear greenish-coloured glass bottles, the sort that might have contained lemonade, and inside was what appeared to be a piece of paper.

It seemed to have been rolled up tightly so that it could be pushed into the bottle via its narrow neck. She could not see whether there was a message on the paper because the part she could see looked as if it bore part of a flowery pattern or design rather than writing. If there was any writing, it would surely be on the inside. When she turned the bottle around, it seemed the pattern covered the entire back of the paper, but when she tried to unscrew the cork, it was too firmly fast. She made absolutely no impression upon it. Clearly it was a job for stronger fingers and so she decided to take the bottle home to Dad. Replacing her sandals and calling for Pip, she walked through the town to her home in Rowan Street. The Youngs lived in a smart semi-detached house, with Dad (Ian) working for the Urban District Council, and so Saturday was his morning off. When she returned home, he had finished his breakfast and was busy in his back garden tending his vegetable crop.

'Dad,' she called excitedly, 'I found this on the beach, a message in a bottle.'

'Really?' he stopped his hoeing and went across to the lawn where she was waiting. 'Where's it come from?'

'I don't know, I can't loosen the cork.'

After a quick look at it, he took it from her and tried to unscrew the cork with his fingers but couldn't secure a firm enough grip and so he said, 'I've a pair of pliers in the shed, they'll do the trick. I don't want to smash it though.'

She followed him into the shed where he found his pliers and used them to gain a strong grip of the top of the cork, held the bottle firmly in the other hand and began to turn it very carefully.

Slowly, he felt the cork begin to turn and

smiled to indicate his success, and soon he had removed it. 'Now,' he said, frowning, 'all I have to do is get this message out! I need something long and thin, like a pencil maybe, to drag it out.' He tried shaking it but it didn't work and so he found a long pencil in his tool box. It had a rubber on the tip. By inserting it through the neck and pressing the rubber against the paper, he was able to man- oeuvre the message ever so slightly, gradually inching it closer to the neck. In time, he succeeded in getting the message out and spread it open on his bench. It was a scrap of torn wallpaper about twice the size of a playing card and it had clearly been pulled off a wall. It was very stiff with fragments of wall- paper paste adhering to it. One edge was straight, as if this had been covering part of the wall near a window frame or doorway, but the rest had irregular tear marks around it. The message was in rather unskilled hand- writing, apparently written with a blunt pencil, and it said, 'Help, please get me out. I am imprisoned here upstairs. Jenny.' And that was all. The spelling was correct, and the writing was joined-up, indicating that the writer was not a very small child.

'Where did you say you found this?' Ian asked his daughter.

She explained precisely which part of the beach she had been walking upon when she'd spotted the bottle, and then he said, 'I think we'd better tell the police about this. I just hope it's not some kind of sick joke.'

'Why, what do you think it means, Dad?'

'I'm not sure, but that looks like a piece of old wallpaper which has been torn off a wall. It's the sort of paper you'd expect in a bedroom, so if it's genuine and really from this girl Jenny, it sounds as if she's locked in a bedroom.'

'You mean she's being kept a prisoner? Like in the olden days?'

'That's what it suggests. But if she is, how could she get this bottle into the sea? And there's no address or date, although it's a local bottle, Hicksons make soft drinks here in Strensford. And why couldn't she raise the alarm in some other way? It's a real puzzle, Jess. Come along, let's take it to the police and see what they think.'

By chance, I was on office duty in Strensford Police Station when Ian and Jessica Young arrived. The regular office duty constable was enjoying his weekly rest day and I was deputizing, taking the opportunity to catch up on some of my paperwork on the office typewriter. Ian came to the counter and plonked the bottle in the hatchway as he told me the story. The piece of wallpaper was in an envelope which he handed over. I listened carefully, asked Jessica a few questions and examined both the paper and the bottle. I saw the name on the bottle – in raised glass letters, it said, 'Hicksons of Strensford', but even so I had to admit, 'I don't know what to make of this, Mr Young. If it's genuine, we'll have to find out where it's come from and why but if it's just some kind of joke we don't want to waste time and resources investigating it. Will you leave it with me for a while? I'll have words with my colleagues, and with the Coastguards to see if they can advise which currents might have brought it ashore. We might be able to find out where it was put into the sea.'

He agreed and said he would look forward to the outcome. When he'd gone, I knocked on the Sergeants' Office door where I knew Sergeant Morris was working and was admitted to tell the story. He listened with a mixture of doubt and concern, wondering whether we should spend time trying to find out more, or whether to disregard it as nothing more than a child's prank. After all, he pointed out, it could have been thrown into the sea at the very place it was found, a prank by someone keen to see what the outcome might be. He also wondered about the value of publicity in the local paper but, as I explained, if this was a genuine cry for help, then publicity could have an adverse effect.

After some discussion, he said, 'Right, Nick, I'll tell you what. First, I don't want you to make an almighty fuss about this, so what I suggest is that you make very discreet inquiries to see if you can establish where and how the bottle got into the sea, where the wallpaper has come from and whether we need to worry officially about the mysterious Jenny. Remember she might be a child, but equally she might be a batty old woman. Or even a daft lad or young woman pretending to be an imprisoned woman. Someone hoping to generate some kind of scare story or publicity. There are all sorts of possibilities. Proceed with great caution – I think that's the advice I would give. But it would be nice to have an answer to all this!'

'I'll do my best,' I promised.

Later that day, when my period of office duty was over, I had four hours still to complete for my shift, and I was allocated no. 1 beat which took me along the harbour on its northern side.

The portion nearest the town centre comprised lots of old cottages, houses and shops squeezed into the smallest of spaces but that part of my beat that afternoon which extended towards the outskirts, albeit along the riverbank, consisted of modern business premises such as boat builders, a caravan salesroom, a garage and several other new enterprises. Among them, however, was the century-old premises of Hicksons Mineral Waters, a ramshackle conglomeration of sheds, offices and warehouses which had been producing soft drinks and lemonade for generations. The premises were surrounded by high wire fencing and gates to deter thieves. I decided to pay them a visit. I would take the bottle too! And while doing that, I slipped the piece of wallpaper into the pocket of my notebook.

When I arrived, the gates were open and I spotted a sign directing me to a reception point. It was an office in one of the wooden sheds and a sign on the door said, 'Knock and Enter'. So I did to find myself standing before a desk bearing a sign saying 'Reception', along with a bell. I pressed the button and a smartly dressed middle-aged woman appeared from next door. Her face registered evident surprise when she saw a policeman standing there, and her hands went up to her face.

'Oh, a policeman! Have we done something wrong?' she giggled.

'Not to my knowledge, but I've an enquiry to make,' and I pulled the bottle from the carrier bag I was using and plonked it on the counter. 'About this.'

'Oooh! One of our new bottles!' she smiled.

'New?' I was intrigued by this. 'How new?'

'A couple of weeks. It's our new design, the shoulders are slimmer than the old one, the neck is a wee bit shorter and the bottle is a fraction taller. It holds the same amount, though, and I think it looks more elegant than the old ones.'

'So what did this contain? It's got a screw top.'

'Lemonade,' she nodded. 'Other soft drinks and less fizzy ones have caps, like some bottles of beer.'

'Ah,' I said. 'So can we say where this one was likely to have been bought, when it was full?'

'Well, normally it might have been difficult but in this case, with the bottle being our new design, it's only on sale at the moment to outlets in Strensford and district. We're gauging the response to it, and if it's favourable we'll introduce it to our other delivery areas, gradually replacing old ones with new ones.'

"So this one would have been sold by you to a customer somewhere in Strensford and district? In the last couple of weeks. That wouldn't be a direct sale to the buyer, would it?'

'No, we sell wholesale to shops, pubs and such places.' By now, her face was showing her curiosity as she added, 'If it had had its sticky label on, I could have told you which area of Strensford it went to. They've got tiny identification marks on them, a sort of delivery code, so the draymen know where each consignment is heading when it leaves the depot.'

'I think it's been in the sea for a while,' I told her. 'That's probably washed it off.'

'Oh, I see. That's a pity, I can't really say which area of town it went to. But can I ask why you are interested in this bottle?'

'It was found on the beach by a child, only this morning,' I said. 'She found it floating in the sea and there was a message inside which makes us feel just a little concerned about the person who wrote the message. There is a suggestion that the person who wrote it is imprisoned in a room of some kind.'

'That's dreadful! Do you think it's possible? Is it true, do you think? Or is it some kind of childish prank?'

'I don't know, there is a certain ring of truth about it all, which is why I'm here, asking these questions.'

'Well, I must say if it's a local bottle, it hasn't got very far, has it?'

'Not a round-the-world trip by any means! But maybe that was the intention of the thrower? To have it found quickly? So when you say it was sold to a shop or pub some-where in Strensford and district, what sort of range does that include?'

'The whole of the town,' she said. 'And all outlets within two miles of the town centre – the post office that is. That's usually the starting point for measuring distances to other places. It means we deliver in some rural areas, and to some isolated places like lonely pubs and even kiosks near the beach. We call it the home run, it's our main one.'

'And would it be possible for me to have a list of the outlets on that run? Then I could visit them to see if they might help me find the person who bought it.'

'Well, yes, under the circumstances I can do that. But it's a tall order, isn't it? Finding out which individual bought just one of our bottles? We sell thousands.'

'Nothing's impossible,' I said. 'The message itself, and the paper it's written on will help too. But the content of the message makes it necessary, it suggests that the person who threw the bottle into the sea could be in danger. I realize it might be a joke or a prank of some kind, but we've got to do our best to check it out.'

'So the person who bought it must have got close enough to the sea to be able to toss the bottle in, without it breaking on rocks and so on? That's not easy for somebody imprisoned in a room!'

'That's an important point,' I agreed. 'It's especially so if the person was unable to get down to the beach or onto the cliffs. If she is being held somewhere – we think it's a woman or girl – it must mean the house or building from which it was thrown was close enough to get the bottle into the sea.'

'There are a lot of houses overlooking the harbour, small old places with the water literally outside the walls. You could drop a bottle from the upper stories of those houses and it would land in the harbour, especially at high tide.'

'Exactly, so where do I start?'

'I'll help all I can, but there's so little to go on. If you'd like to wait now, though, I can run off a copy of our delivery list on the

Gestetner, it'll take about five minutes.'

'I'll wait,' I said.

In the far corner of the reception area, she indicated a couple of easy chairs with a table in front of them; the table contained a variety of magazines and several bottles of their products, along with some clean glasses.

'Help yourself to a drink,' she invited. 'They're all non-alcoholic, by the way!'

As I waited, I noticed, on the wall, an Ordnance Survey map of the district and it showed the delivery areas in this part of Yorkshire, and I could see that the company covered a massive area. Strensford looked small by comparison but as I examined the map, I realized that the new bottles were limited to a very small area in comparison with their entire distribution coverage – but that small patch had a lot of outlets. It would take days or even weeks to visit each one. Another thought occurred to me too. There was another way of getting a bottle into the sea – that was by dropping it into a river or stream which flowed into the sea. And lots of houses in rural areas overlooked such rivers and streams.

I realized that my second line of inquiry must be with personnel of HM Coastguard who might be able to help with the currents off that coast, possibly suggesting a place where the bottle might have entered the sea in order to he washed up on Strensford sands. Then I would visit a wallpaper shop.

The helpful receptionist, whose name I learned was Linda Britten, re-appeared with her list of customers in Strensford and district, pointed out several of particular interest such as larger places like motels and Strensford Spa while adding some were merely little kiosks near the beach, open only during the summer holiday season with moderately small orders.

I thanked her for her help and promised I would return with the result of my efforts, then left to head for the coast-guard station. If they couldn't help me, then perhaps some of the local inshore fishermen might. It was a long climb up the cliff path to the High Ness where the coastguard station was situated but it was one of our regular calling points. It was considered useful for the police to know the personnel of HM Coastguard, particularly if they had to work together in the future and so, when I arrived, I was pleased to see Arthur Judson on duty. A thickset, bearded man in his mid-fifties, with the look of a seaman about him, he and I would often have long chats whenever I had to work night duty on this beat. I think my visits, and those of my colleagues, broke the monotony of his lonely watch over the dark North Sea.

This afternoon, however, it was daylight when I joined him on a chair at his desk with its array of switches, lights, radio receivers, microphones, lists of the flags and symbols of international recognition for ships of every kind. On one wall was a map of the sea bed off Strensford which depicted all its con- cealed rocks, hollows, hills and even some larger wrecks which had been there for cen- turies. Others, however, were from the two recent world wars. The table of tides for the entire north-east coast was also prominent but ahead was a wall of thick glass which pro- duced a panoramic vista across the waves from the cliff top. The huge windows ensured that every inch of the sea could be seen to the north, west and south, and standing in the centre were the official binoculars.

On my first visit, I remember thinking it was a telescope because it stood on a plinth while being moveable up and down, and from side to side, ranging from north to south. But when I was offered a peep through, I realized it was a massive pair of high-powered and very sophisticated binoculars, ones which could read the name, registration number and other details of a ship many miles out to sea. One bonus when visiting the coastguard station was that there was always fresh tea in the pot and so, as I joined Arthur over a cup, we chatted about nothing in particular and then I referred to my query. In particular, I wanted his advice on which current or currents would bring a bottle ashore.

'Oh, I've got some charts which will help,' he said, pulling from beneath his counter what looked like a large-scale photographic album. Inside, however, were charts of the coast and seabed. 'These show the prevailing currents,' he said. 'Some are very deep and others near the surface, but even if we think we know their routes, they can be affected by the tides, atmospheric pressure, the salinity of the water, the temperature of the water in summer and winter, the wind and, of course, the depth of the sea at a particular place and time. We've gained a lot of knowledge from things like driftwood and wrecks, and in fact special drift bottles are often used to identify the routes of currents. What is important to the currents off-shore at this point is the prevailing wind, the configuration of the seabed and the coast.

And, of course, the input of fresh water from rivers and streams coming from the land also has an effect.'

'Oh,' I said, deciding to press him for an answer. 'The bottle in question came ashore at Strensford this morning. It was found before nine o'clock, still in the water. I know it's a local bottle, one made here in Strensford and brought into use within the last couple of weeks. It had been in the sea long enough for the label to be washed off. What I would like to know, if possible, is where it came from. North or south, for example.'

'Oh, the north, there's no doubt about that. The wind this morning was coming off the sea, so that would help to drive the bottle inshore, but the tide and the currents would have swept it out to sea earlier. So imagine the bottle moving out to sea during the night, taken there by a combination of prevailing wind, tide and current, and then being swept ashore this morning on the rising tide, and almost being swept back out to sea on the ebb tide, had that lass not found it.'

'I think it was thrown into the sea from a house bedroom,' I told Arthur, giving my reasons.

'In that case, it would be tossed into a

stream or river,' he said. 'Here, look along the coast with those glasses, you'll see there's no houses on the coast to the north. But there's a few streams entering the sea to the north – all within a couple of miles of here.'

He was right. Once away from the cliffs of Strensford, the coastline comprised cliffs, fields and open countryside with several farms deep inland, but no cottages or houses actually on the shore.

'So you'd suggest someone threw it into a stream which ran into the sea, just along the coast from here?'

'Bearing in mind all the factors, yes. Let's have a look at some more charts, where the becks enter the sea. Fresh water coming into the sea produces its own currents before it merges with the salt water, and there's the difference in temperature to consider, and the tide at the time, and the wind direction ... ah, here we are.'

He flipped through his book of charts until he came to one which looked promising. He said nothing for a while as he studied it, checking his own records of wind direction and strength, the times of high tide, the temperature and atmospheric pressure.

'Right, Nick,' he said eventually. 'Now I can't guarantee any of this, we're dealing with nature's variables all the time but I'd say that bottle got into the sea by floating down Underdale Beck. It runs straight off the moors and across the beach into the sea, there's no cliff or waterfall, and if the tide was ebbing, it would soon be carried out to sea, and then winds and currents would fetch it into Strensford Bay, and the incoming tide, with a bit of help from the wind, would carry it inshore. That's my guess – and it is a guess, but I reckon it could have happened like that.'

'I wonder if there are any houses close to that beck?' I asked.

'I've maps of the area, large scale. On rolls under the desk...'

And so he produced a map which included Underdale Beck and sure enough, there was a lonely and very isolated farmhouse standing beside the stream. On the map it was shown as Underdale Mill.

'I think I should pay them a discreet visit,' I said.

'If that doesn't work, I can't offer much else, but if you've problems you think I can help with, then come back for another chat. It helps pass the time in here. It gets mighty boring as you can imagine.'

And so I made a note of the mill's name,

but as my shift was almost over, I had to return to the police station and book off duty. I didn't think I would be permitted to claim overtime for what might turn out to be a hoax or joke. Nonetheless, I still had the piece of wallpaper and was due to return to Strensford for further duty the following day; I would then continue my inquiries. The following day I reminded Sergeant Morris of the progress I had made, and of my wish to continue with my inquiries, and he agreed. He even said I could borrow the station car to drive out to Underdale Mill – in fact he said he would accompany me, but suggested I first complete my inquiries into the piece of torn wallpaper.

Strensford has several shops – six in total – which sell decorating materials and wall-papers and so I began a systematic tour of them all, showing them the paper in question. Even from visiting only the first three, however, it was clear that the piece was several years old. It was by no means a modern design nor was the paper from a modern manufacturer. Every shopkeeper said so, one suggesting it was about twenty-five years old or more, possibly pre-war, and all agreed it was the sort of floral design one would expect to find in a bedroom in the

1930s. All added that the remnants of adhesive also suggested it was very old – it was not a case of using modern adhesive to hang an old wallpaper.

I went to all the shops because I had further questions to ask each one – could they remember selling the paper I showed them, and if so, to whom? In fact, the fifth shop I visited still sold that make of wallpaper, albeit in up-to-date designs, but the owner, a man in his sixties who had been in the shop for more than forty years, could not recall selling that particular piece. He did agree, however, that it was at least twenty-five years old and probably more. And so I concluded my inquiry at all six shops, my only success being to learn the probable age of the wallpaper and its likely use. None could throw any light upon who Jenny might be and none could recall selling the piece.

I returned to the police station to inform Sergeant Morris and he expressed his pleasure at what I had achieved and then said we should both drive out to Underdale Mill. A check of the electoral register showed it was occupied by Reuben, Mary and Catherine Cole but there were no details of their age, occupation or marital status. There was no Jenny, I noted. A further check in the directory did not produce a telephone number for them either and a look through the police station records did not suggest the family was known to the police for any reason. They had not come to our notice for good or bad reasons. The mill did not appear to be active either, otherwise we would have been aware of its role within the Division; it was probably one of many derelict water-mills in the vicinity. We checked the map before leaving and it reinforced the coast-guard's opinion that the mill was very remote but we found an access road, albeit unsurfaced according to the map.

And so, with me at the wheel, the Strensford sergeant and I sallied forth on our very odd mission, taking the bottle and paper with us. We drove for a couple of miles out of town, with the coast road rising to a considerable height above sea-level to provide wonderful views, and then we arrived at the unsurfaced lane leading towards the mill. It was not signposted but a check of our map told us we were heading in the right direction, which was a gentle downhill track heading towards the shoreline. The mill was midway between the coast road and that shoreline, and according to the map, the track halted at the mill and the buildings which surrounded it. A stream ran from the moors, flowing almost parallel with the track before weaving through the buildings where it had once operated the millwheel. Beyond the buildings, it descended steadily to flow into the sea by crossing the beach at ground level rather than a waterfall. So was that the site of our bottle throwing?

With the sea as a backcloth to our view we chugged steadily down the lane, our shining black car glinting in the sunlight. The little Ford Prefect did not carry POLICE signs or a blue light, being merely the station run-about, consequently if it was being observed on its arrival, it might generate some interest but not as much as it might if it was recognized as an approaching police vehicle. Within minutes, the bulky outline of the mill came into view. Commanding stunning views across the North Sea and down the coastline, it was built of local stone with stone tiles on the roof and it had a rather squat appearance which was designed to cope with the fierce coastal climate.

As we drew closer, we could see the mill-wheel on the side of the house but there was no sign of people, livestock or domestic ani-mals like dogs and cats, and then we entered a wide stony area with the house door ahead. The overall appearance was one of neglect and dereliction, such a pity for a handsome building on such a beautiful site: old items of farm machinery, domestic furniture, a mangle, several carts and even a couple of old rusting cars stood in front of the house. I eased the car to a halt on the stony area, and we climbed out; as I did so, I caught sight of a movement in one of the upper-storey windows but it vanished even before I could decide whether it was a man or a woman, or merely a fluttering curtain. As we walked towards the front door, devoid of paint and in need of some attention to its woodwork, I realized we had to cross a small footbridge. It led up to the front door – which meant those upper rooms were directly above the stream which flowed quickly past the house before being guided into the millrace. Even at this point, the water was a couple of feet deep. With Sergeant Morris standing a little way behind me and gazing at the windows, I rapped on the door, shouting 'Hello' because there was no doorbell. In such a large house, I wondered if my knocking would be heard, for other than the fleeting glimpse at that upper window there was no sign of anyone around the premises. If no one responded, the next trick was to open the door and shout, then do a tour of the premises to see if there was another entrance.

But my shout produced a result.

A stooped old woman appeared. Grey-haired and pale faced, she looked anywhere between sixty and ninety. She was also very frail and unkempt.

She opened the door and blinked in the sunlight.

'Yes?'

'Mrs Cole?' I asked.

'Yes?'

'I am PC Rhea from Aidensfield, although I'm working in Strensford at the moment, and this is Sergeant Morris from Strensford.'

'Yes?'

'Can we have a word with you?'

'Yes.'

She made no effort to invite us inside and left us standing on the little footbridge with the water rushing beneath, so I produced the bottle and wallpaper from the carrier bag.

'Have you seen these before? A lemonade bottle, one of Hicksons from Strensford, and a piece of wallpaper.'

She peered at the items and I wondered about the quality of her eyesight, and then she nodded. 'I wondered where that bottle had got to.'

'Really?' I wondered how she recognized one bottle from another but didn't press the matter just yet. Instead, I showed her the wallpaper, displaying its pattern but not the message inside.

'Yes,' she nodded fiercely. 'That's off our Kate's wall, I recognize it, there's a big patch where she tore it off. I wondered where it had gone, it wasn't there when I went in to clean up. I guessed she must have tossed it out of the window.'

'So who is Kate?'

'My daughter. She's ill, you know, always has been ever since she was a tot. Never goes out, we daren't let her out, she spends all day in her room,' and she pointed up to the windows above the door. I looked up and was in time to see another fleeting glimpse of someone or something moving.

'Can she talk to us?'

'Not very well.'

'Mrs Cole,' said Sergeant Morris. 'Someone found this bottle in the sea at Strensford, yesterday morning. It suggests someone is held prisoner and is asking for help.'

'She does it all the time, Sergeant. Come along, you'd better come and see for yourself.'

She stepped back into the beautifully panelled entrance hall with its stone floor and led us across to the corner where a winding staircase led to the first floor. We followed her onto a landing with bare wooden floorboards and she took us to a door, shouted, 'Kate, there's someone to see you,' and went in ahead of us. I noted the door was not locked. Inside, we saw a deformed woman, bent and crippled like some old crone from the middle ages, and it took only a couple of seconds for us to realize she was both physically and mentally handicapped. She was dressed in a delicate and very pretty long pink frock, the sort that might have been popular in Victorian times, and her light brown hair was long and in ringlets. She looked like something from a fable of long ago.

I guessed she would be in her late forties or even her fifties.

'Kate, this is Sergeant Morris and PC Rhea, they have come to see you.'

The woman produced a toothless grin which spoilt her pretty face, but no words emerged, other than a type of grunt.

'Kate,' continued Mrs Cole. 'Did you throw your lemonade bottle out of the window?'

We were rewarded with another grin and

grunt, and the same result happened when she asked Kate about the message on the wallpaper. I was now aware of the matching paper on her bedroom wall, with several bare patches where pieces had been stripped off.

'The message was spelt correctly,' I said to Mrs Cole, adding, 'but it was apparently signed by someone called Jenny.'

'She reads a lot, PC Rhea, and one of her books is a story about a girl called Jenny who was a prisoner on a ship and threw a bottle into the sea in the hope someone would find it and rescue her.'

'So she can read and write?'

'She writes very well, I think she learns a lot from her reading.'

'Have you thought about getting help?' asked Sergeant Morris. 'You seem to be taking on a lot, all on your own.'

'Reuben helps, he's my husband, he's out working now, he earns a few pounds helping on nearby farms. We don't spend much, Sergeant. We never go anywhere but we've always prided ourselves on looking after Kate ourselves.'

'A big commitment.'

'Yes, but it's family and so you do your best. We would never want her taken away from us.'

'But sometimes a helping hand is necessary.'

'I am aware of that, now we're getting older. One day, she'll be left all on her own...'

'There's no need for that, she can be looked after,' said the Sergeant. 'Would you like us to contact a mental welfare officer and get her to visit you? You needn't be alone in this, Mrs Cole, and Kate would not be taken away from you, not without your consent.'

I realized we were chatting within hearing distance of Kate and I also realized she understood everything we were saying; the movements of her hands and eyes, and the grunts she uttered, all indicated she would like to get some kind of professional help.

'Would you like these gentlemen to arrange for some help, Kate?' asked her mother.

Kate grew excited and grunted a lot, waving her arms and nodding and so her mum smiled and I could see tears in her eyes.

'No one's offered help before, but that's our fault, we've never asked. We've never known who to ask. We are very innocent, living so far from civilization ... so what will you do now?'

Sergeant Morris said, 'When I return to Strensford, I'll talk to the local mental welfare officer and explain the situation. They'll come along for a chat with you and Kate – and your husband, of course. I think you'll be surprised and pleased at the treatments and facilities which are available for girls like Kate.'

'It was different in our day,' said Mrs Cole. 'We just hid people like Kate from view.'

'Not any more. People with Kate's problems can learn to lead a very full and active life. Come along, PC Rhea, back to base. Well, Mrs Cole, Kate's message in a bottle has produced a result, eh?'

On our way to the station, we didn't speak very much. We thought about the years of isolation and boredom endured by Kate with no human contact other than her loving parents. I was delighted that her message in the bottle had led to her own release from a particularly terrible form of unintended imprisonment.

I received a report of another curious discovery on the beach, this time on the rocks at the foot of the cliffs which overlooked the southern part of Strensford Bay. It was a small rowing boat, more of a dinghy really because it was capable of carrying no more than two people, and there was no sign of a paddle or oar. It was the sort of light craft one might find carried by cabin cruisers and other small pleasure boats, or even towed behind as happened in some cases. It was the type of craft the crew could use to escape from a sinking ship, or more likely to row themselves ashore when the water was too shallow for the larger parent boat to be moored.

A dog walker, a local man, had spotted the dinghy during his early morning outing along the cliff top and upon his return had alerted the police because he feared there were human casualties on those same rocks. If the little dinghy had been swept ashore in heavy seas – and there had been heavy seas during the previous night – there was an even chance that someone had been aboard at the time. And so we had to launch a search of the rocks, pools and caves at the foot of the cliffs, and we had to do so before high tide. Once the tide rose, it would cover the rocks, flood the pools and fill the cliff-base caves with water up to fourteen feet deep. It would also sweep away any dead bodies which might be lying among those rocks. The rocks extended about three hundred yards into the sea and about half a mile in length beneath the cliffs into an adjoining bay which had a sandy beach. Even from the cliff top, it was easy to spot a body lying on the sand but it was very difficult to see one among the rocks. A very careful search was necessary.

Before heading out to commence our work, however, we contacted both the coastguard and our own force control room to ascertain whether or not any ship or boat had been in trouble recently or whether any mayday or SOS calls had been received. None had. According to official records, therefore, there had been no recent disasters in the North Sea off our coastline.

I was a member of the small search party which was speedily mustered to search those rocks, pools and caves. The faster we worked, the more chance there was of salvaging the dinghy before the tide swept it out to sea once more. Apart from that, it might yield some evidence of its origins or a reason for it being beached there.

The search party comprised Sergeant Morris, myself and two town constables, plus one special who had volunteered for this kind of task. We gathered at the end of the east pier from where steps went down to the beach below the cliff and then we could walk to the location on smooth sands before clambering and searching among the rocks. Sergeant Morris knew the coastline intimately and quickly allocated a specific area to each of us. Each had a rough square of rocks reaching from the edge of the water to the foot of the cliffs and he directed us to quarter our own area and make a detailed search for an hour. Then we would halt and rendezvous so that further instructions could be issued, if necessary. He reminded us that the tide would soon turn and begin to flow so we must be on constant alert for that, and he told us that beneath some of those rocks were large cavities and deep pools, any of which were large enough to conceal a human body. There were several caves at the base of the cliff too, all having been scooped out of the softer rock by the action of the water and these could easily contain a body. All of us would do a good job.

First, though, we all stood in a group and examined the little dinghy which was perched somewhat precariously on one flattish rock but wedged between another two. It would be impossible to remove it manually although the rising water would free it with little trouble – but where would it go from here? It was built of wood and shaped rather like a small rowing boat, but rather more rounded. There was a single wooden seat in the centre; it had no back and was nothing more than a wooden plank crossing from port to starboard. There was no rudder and no oars or paddles.

The little boat was painted green with red around the top, and there was a long piece of coiled rope beneath the seat with one end attached to a brass fitting on the tiny bowsprit. Overall, it seemed to be in very good condition. On both its sides, near the bows, was the name DAPHNE in large white lettering but no other form of identification. We did not know whether Daphne was the owner's name, the name of the dinghy or its parent craft. But the boat contained nothing else, consequently there was nothing which would indicate its source or owner.

We set about our search with due diligence, the air being filled with the scent of seaweed, wet sand and the saltiness of the atmosphere which some people mistakenly believe to be ozone. It wasn't an easy task due to the slipperiness of the rocks and the covering of seaweed, while a lot of space between the rocks was still filled with trapped water. There was the inevitable detritus, a curious mixture of everything from oddly shaped pieces of wood and battered drinks crates to old shoes and ladies' underwear via discarded plastic containers and even a deckchair and dead crow. The sea always managed to wash this kind of rubbish into nooks and crannies along the shoreline, only for the next tide to sweep it out again and deposit it elsewhere. In spite of our care, however, we did not find any sign of human remains.

After a couple of hours, Sergeant Morris decided we could do no more. We had literally swept the shoreline along the full length of the base of the cliffs, but furthermore, the tide was coming in and already filling pools among rocks only yards away.

It was now time for us to depart for the safety of dry land but first, one of our officers tied the dinghy to a loose rock, using the rope left inside it, and he allowed enough slack for it to ride the tide. That would secure it until a decision was made about its disposal and it would prevent it getting smashed to matchwood on the rocks.

At Sergeant Morris's command, we hurried from our task and regrouped at the end of the pier.

'Well, lads, that's it.' He sounded relieved that we hadn't discovered human remains. 'I'll return to the office and give the coastguard a call to let him know the outcome, but I know he'll keep watch with those binoculars of his, and if there is a body anywhere, my guess is that he'll spot it.'

'So what happens to the dinghy?' I asked.

'It's not going to be easy getting it off the rocks,' he admitted. 'But that's not our responsibility. However, it is found property so I will enter it in our found property register, naming the finder as that chap who spotted it when he was walking his dog. If it's not claimed within three months, it will be his. Then he can do what he wants with it.'

And so that dog walker found himself the owner of a dinghy but he left it moored on its individual rock, riding out each high tide until the completion of three months. Other than being filled with water from time to time, it suffered no harm or damage. When the police informed the dog walker that the dinghy was now his property because no claimant had come forward, he decided to advertise it for sale.

I discovered later that a seafaring man with a large cabin cruiser bought it from the dog walker because his wife was called Daphne. He moored his large boat some distance offshore near the rocks and managed to get a line to DAPHNE at low tide. And then, when the tide rose, he gently tugged DAPHNE free from her resting place and she followed his boat out to sea like a happy pup following a big dog.

And that was the end of DAPHNE. She vanished over the horizon into the sunset and was never seen again. To this day we have no idea where she came from.

CHAPTER 3

Strensford's location in a sheltered cove between high cliffs overlooking the North Sea was outstanding. There was a harbour which was always busy with fishing boats, pleasure craft and the occasional cargo ship, while the River Tordsay, often brown with fresh water, flowed from the heights of the moors and passed through the harbour before entering the sea from between twin piers. Sea water and fresh water mingled in the middle of that harbour, often to produce an amazing blend of colours especially in winter or times of flooding. A true meeting of the waters. Blue, grey brown and clear water fought for dominance while flocks of herring gulls and black-headed gulls soared over-head, forever wheeling and always screaming, constantly on the lookout for titbits offered by tourists.

Ancient stone houses, some comprising nothing more than a single room downstairs and a bedroom above, were crammed together as they clung to the cliff sides above the harbour like a colony of bats protecting one another from the cold. Often, I wondered whether those primitive houses had any foundations or whether they simply sat on the cliffside like garden huts or henhouses. They appeared to lean against each other for support, with the ever-present unstable and rather loose earth and rocks above them always a threat. The cliffs were never totally stable; they were always on the move and large chunks of stone had been known to tumble down and smash through windows of kitchens and even bedrooms, fortunately without serious injury or loss of life.

There were two parts to the town, the old and the new.

The older part of Strensford, haphazardly built on both sides of the river beneath matching cliffs which formed the valley, boasted a town centre which was known for its medieval town hall perched on top of stone pillars. There was a small marketplace beneath which overlapped into the surrounding cobbled square and there was also a market cross. This was all set amid a network of narrow streets and alleys. Pretty shops with bow windows were enhanced by old inns as dark as night inside which ancient men would smoke clay pipes and sup pints of dark brown ale while discussing events in town, or grumbling about the state of the weather, the herring grounds or the price of fuel for the fishing fleet. Between those buildings, there would be unexpected tiny open squares with flagstones, reminiscent of Dickensian times, and sometimes with flowers in pots or in window boxes. There were no gardens here; these people lived very close to one another, like rabbits in a warren, so plant pots and window boxes were used to brighten their homes.

The very different new part of the town was on the west cliff top and after an initial Victorian boom of tourism when crescents and arcades of splendid, expensive houses were built, with the inevitable hotels and railway station, more modern estates were constructed before and after the Second World War. Those modern streets with shops, offices and wider roads were built to accommodate motor vehicles, something the builders of the old town had not foreseen and so 'new' Strensford could cope with the growing influx of day-trippers and visitors. Most of the visitors were content to spend all day on the wide, sandy beach but some liked to explore the old town; few, if any, explored the new town. They merely parked their cars and buses there.

Strensford's future might not be in everyone wanting to see the distinctive tiny dwelling houses and ancient market square; some visitors might expect modern trends to replace the historic atmosphere, such delights as nightclubs, entertainment centres and twee shops selling rubbish among tawdry souvenirs.

But whatever their hopes and desires, an influx of tourists would bring business into the town, so vital if it was to sustain its population, for until the first war it had depended almost entirely upon the fishing industry. Even though fleets came to Strensford from Scotland, Holland and Northern Europe, and even if supplies of fish like herring, cod, white fish, crabs and lobsters were plentiful at that time, wise old men felt that Strensford's dependence upon the sea could not be guaranteed for ever. It was known that fish stocks were dwindling, probably from over-fishing in other parts of the North Sea, and so the town needed another form of industry which would provide much-needed revenue on a regular basis. Surely it could learn from its earlier tourist boom? If the Victorians had seen fit to travel by train to Strensford, surely modern man in his motor car could be tempted, not necessarily to spend an entire week or fortnight in the resort. He and his family could come for the day and so, with plenty to offer sightseers and visitors, Strensford began to embrace day-trippers while encouraging them to spend generously. The town council had the benefit of a skilled publicity man who generated articles and photographs in all manner of newspapers and magazines, concentrating on those which served the East and West Ridings of Yorkshire as well as the north-east of England, i.e. areas around Middlesbrough, Durham and Newcastle.

All those densely populated areas were within easy driving distance and so people began to explore the town, first as a trickle but later as a flood – which is why extra police officers, such as myself, were required at the busiest times. But it was especially the old town and harbourside.

In addition to providing valuable free publicity, the presence of film-makers generated work as extras for many of the townspeople.

Sometimes the authorities, such as the police, fire, ambulance and local council, were informed by a film company that they would be in town for a particular period, and on occasions a uniformed presence was necessary if roads had to be closed officially or if disruption in public places was likely to occur. When filming took place on private premises, of course, the authorities were rarely told because it was usually not necessary and on many such occasions, the presence of the police was likewise not required. However, when filming – known as shooting in the profession – was undertaken in the streets or public places, a police officer would generally be present to assist with traffic control and help the production team complete their task. There were the inevitable grumbles from some locals and visitors who saw this activity as an unwelcome intrusion but, in general, film-making produced a positive and favourable impact upon the district, both when famous faces were spotted in town and when the final result reached the screen.

Many police officers on duty during film-making worked on their days off which meant they were not taken away from normal duties. They were paid at overtime rates and the police authority was adequately reimbursed by the film company. In other words, it cost the rate payer and tax payer nothing while boosting the attraction of the location in question. In all, a good investment.

In the case of Strensford, this additional opportunity to earn extra cash was generally offered to the local constables, not to incomers like myself, but from time to time, a chance did arise for an outside officer to work with a film crew on his or her day off. With four fast-growing children, I needed as much money as I could earn and so when I received a telephone call, asking if I would be prepared to work with a film crew at Strensford on my day off, I seized the opportunity. And so it was that, at six o'clock one Tuesday morning in early summer, I found myself in Strensford old town where the marketplace had been commandeered by a film crew.

The necessary permission had been obtained from the council and police for the marketplace and the nearby approach roads to be temporarily closed to the public, although the film crew would open them when required for the benefit of the local inhabitants while filming was not actually under way. My job was to ensure that peace was maintained throughout the filming and to deal with any motorists or others who might become obnoxious, and of course, to liaise between the production team and any member of the public who might have an urgent and valid reason for passing through.

News of the presence of the crew had been published in the *Strensford Gazette* and also on posters in shops, pubs and public buildings, and so it was presumed that all the local people were aware of the disruption which would occur.

When I arrived, the market square had been transformed. It had been dressed to appear as if it was set in the 1920s with a small vegetable and fruit market of that period complete with stalls, stallholders, produce, customers and contemporary vehicles, both horse-drawn and motors. There were other stalls too, such as clothes, shoes, baby wear, fish, meat and even flowers and their seeds. Actors had been commissioned to take the part of the key stallholders but extras were filling the roles of others, including most customers who did nothing more than wander around the market to inspect the stalls. The lead characters were a young man and woman, lovers whose story was being told in the film, and in these scenes they were customers visiting the market, an essential part of the storyline. These were played by professional artistes, and everyone, including the extras, was in period dress.

The storyline involved a romance between the daughter of a Yorkshire fisherman from a town like Strensford and a hard-working but unsuccessful watercolour artist who had come temporarily to the town to seek inspiration for some seascapes and pictures of sailing ships in full sail. The girl was from a hard-working but poor background and her parents did not believe that an impoverished would-be artist would make her a suitable husband. Several market scenes were scheduled to be completed during the day because this was the favourite meeting place of the young lovers.

I looked forward to this unusual duty, and learned that the working title of the film was *Tide of Romance*, based on a book by a local author. Before the cameras began to roll, assistants employed by the film company went to their posts at all the entrances to the market square, their job being to halt any unauthorized or curious people who might try to enter the set, and also to ensure silence and stillness during the shooting. There would be last-minute adjustments to the make-up and costumes of the cast and extras, final checks of actions and words, re-runs of the choreographed movements of the extras around the stalls, a check of the cameras and sound equipment and then that long wait until the director called 'action' when everything and everyone was supposed to work in cohesion to the well-rehearsed plan. Everything would be concentrated on the scenes being played out before us and, if things did not work out as planned, there would be several 'takes'. To achieve a perfect result in take one was the dream of every director.

After discussions with the production team, I decided to place myself on the busiest street leading into the marketplace. That was where problems were most likely to arise. Film production officials were in position on all corners of the market too but the street in which I would be present brought all vehicular traffic into the market square, and beyond was a dead end. The fact that there was no through-traffic made things much easier to control, the only way out of the market being to make a circuit of the square and exit via another street. The only people likely to want to progress beyond the market square, towards the dead end, would be local residents and perhaps an occasional delivery vehicle.

Hopefully, no emergency would arise where noisy vehicles like fire appliances or ambulances were required. There seemed to be a lot of waiting around as the final preparations were made and then, once everyone was in position, the signal for silence was given and the director shouted 'action'. As take one got underway with the market square coming to life with noise, chatter and bustle, plus the loud and repetitive calls of the stallholders, I watched with undisguised fascination and then a little elderly woman pushed past me, saying, 'Oh dear, I'm late. I'm late.'

I was on the point of halting her when I realized she was part of the action. Made-up to look as if she was in her early eighties, she was rather stooped and dressed in 1920s clothing complete with little black ankle-length boots, a shawl and a hairnet. With a wicker basket hanging from her left arm, she scurried across to the vegetable stall and I heard her say, 'Three pounds of potatoes, please.'

The man smiled and weighed them, put them in a brown paper bag and handed them to her, saying, 'Tuppence luv.' She delved into her basket, found her purse and extracted two pennies.

'They're a bit cheap, aren't they?' she said quite loudly. 'I hope they're all right. I hope you're not selling me rubbish.'

And then I realized something was wrong. There was some kind of commotion, the source of which was unknown to me, and the director was waving his hands as he indicated silence; from his gestures, I realized he was telling the cast and crew to ignore the problem and continue. And so they did.

I watched the little old lady scampering around the stalls with one of the cameras concentrating upon her as she bought what appeared to be her weekly requirements, passing caustic comments about the condition of some of the produce, and then she turned and made her way back towards the exit at which I was standing. Meanwhile, the extras were moving around the stalls, pretending to be shoppers. As the elderly lady reached the exit, the male and female leads appeared from behind me and once they were in the market, the cameras picked them up. As they entered the set, however, the little old lady said to them, 'Good-morning, if you're new here, just watch that chap on the fruit stall, his apples are a bit on the soft side in my opinion, I don't think his oranges are ripe and I wouldn't touch his onions with a barge pole.' And then she departed.

Fascinated by her realistic portrayal of a 1920s shopper, I watched her potter along the street, and then she disappeared down one of the alleys, out of sight and out of mind. I guessed she would now make her way back to the house which had been hired as a green room for the cast. When I turned my attention back to the filming, the young lovers were standing together close to the town hall's pillars and were exchanging words of romance and love. And then came the call 'cut' and everything stopped. At that point, most of the cast and crew collapsed into bouts of laughter.

Standing away from the centre of things, I had no idea what had amused them but now there was a regrouping and positioning of cast, extras and crew for take two. Preparation for this would take a few minutes and as it was going on, the assistant director, a man called John Elliot, came over to speak to me.

'Constable.' He was a dapper individual with long black hair and a neat line in velvet suits and purple suede shoes. 'Would you know who that little woman is? The one who bought the potatoes?'

'No idea,' I admitted. 'Is she famous? Should I recognize her?'

'Well, with you being a local bobby, I thought you might know who she is. She's not one of ours, by the way. Not an actress or an extra. We've no idea who she is, we've never seen her before.'

'Really? I thought she was part of the scene. She was dressed for it!'

'Yes, but she's not with us. She walked in as if she owned the place, bought some fruit and vegetables, made some cracks about the state of the stuff on sale and left. We decided to keep the cameras rolling because she was so natural and so good, especially her comments about the fruit and vegetables. Now I have to find her and get permission to use that clip of her, and pay her a fee for a speaking part!'

'Well, I'm not local to Strensford, I've been drafted in just for today but when she left, she turned down that alley,' and I indicated the route she had taken.

'Well, I haven't time to go chasing her now but when we break for coffee at ten, I'll see if she lives there. Thanks.'

'I'm sorry if I let her through when I

shouldn't have done...'

'No problem, it's not your job; we've our own stewards who should be watching for that sort of thing but she caught everyone by surprise. Leave it for now, I'll see if I can find her later.'

'There are private houses down there,' I told him.

'Thanks. The trouble is we'll have to do the other takes without her but a spot of clever editing might make sure she's included. We all thought she was great, which is why we went along with it.'

Take two followed without the little woman, then take three, four and five with cast and crew showing the remarkable patience and professionalism for which film crews are renowned. There was a half-hour coffee break at ten o'clock and I was invited to join everyone at their mobile canteen where I discovered the little old lady was the focus of their conversation. Clearly, she had been a hit with everyone who had seen her in action. I learned that John Elliot had gone to see if he could find her and much to everyone's surprise and joy, he returned with her on his arm, like a groom walking his bride down the aisle. She was still dressed in the outfit she had worn earlier and a huge cheer arose from the gathering. I could see she was bewildered by it all but John held up his hands for silence and stood on a beer crate to address us.

'Hi everyone, I'd like you to meet Lilian, Lilian Franklyn who lives just around the corner, behind this marketplace. I've explained to her just what's going on but she thought it was Wednesday which is normal market day. She wondered why prices were so low and expressed her opinion in a good old-fashioned Yorkshire manner. However we will pay her as a speaking extra but we would like her to join us for the rest of the day just in case we need her services again! How about that, Lilian? Can you stay and have lunch with us?'

'How much will that cost?' she asked. 'I've only got my pension you know.'

'Nothing, it's free. And we'll give you something for your starring role. Would ten pounds be all right?'

'Ten pounds? That's more than a week's wages for a working man!'

'Well, you did us proud. So here you are, ten pounds so we can use your piece in the picture we're making. And we'll make sure you see it when it's finished.' And he passed ten pound notes to her.

'Well, I'm not sure I want to see myself up

there on a big screen: it's bad enough looking in the mirror on a morning! I'm not
exactly what you'd call a raving beauty. But
of course you can use me, if I can keep those
potatoes and things. It's not everybody who
gets their picture taken by the movies when
they're buying their weekly groceries.'

'Well once we've finished filming here
today, you can have as much fruit and vegetables as you want.'

And so little Lilian, who in fact was almost
eighty-two years old and unmarried, became a film star quite by accident and when
the picture was released, the film company
told several local papers so she got a second
dose of fame and publicity. But she never
bought any modern clothes. She was well
known in the town as the lady who never
bought new clothes; she insisted on trying
to wear out those in her wardrobe.

That was not the only occasion when
members of the public have mistaken film
props for the genuine article.

On other similar occasions in Strensford, I
saw a man try to make a telephone call from
a false kiosk, another did likewise in a fake
AA box on a moorland road; one lady
posted her letters in a fake pillar box and a
couple of ramblers once boarded a film

company's bus as it waited in a side-street until required for a scene.

One of the funniest such incidents – and potentially a very serious matter – occurred at York Races when Her Majesty was paying a private visit to one of the meetings. She had insisted on the minimum of fuss and proto-col, with none of the trappings of an official visit and so she mingled with the crowd in the grandstand on the famous Knavesmire. Obviously, her attendants had to be present, along with plain-clothes police officers and security men along with other officials but in fact, few of the racegoers knew that Her Majesty was among the crowd.

It was perhaps unfortunate that a local television company was shooting scenes for a drama production during that very meet-ing, few racegoers realizing that, in addition to Her Majesty, there was also a film crew at work among the crowd. The actors and extras were there too, the idea being that the racecourse scenes should be made as rea-listic as possible. The presence of cameras, microphones and lights was not unusual on the racecourse, especially when the meeting was being shown live on television, con-sequently few of the punters gave them a second thought.

Matters were compounded, however, because one of the scenes to be shot during that meeting was a police chase. Six or seven uniformed police officers were going to hunt a dangerous armed criminal among the crowd, with a finale showing them pouncing heavily upon him.

That scene would take place at the rails near the finishing post while a race was being run. It was supposed to be a very dramatic scene. In fact, it turned out to be more dramatic then expected because the real policemen on duty spotted the villain with his gun and then noticed what looked like real officers in hot pursuit, all within a few yards of Her Majesty. Unfortunately, the real police had not been told about the filming. At the sight of a fracas near Her Majesty, there was an immediate security alert with every genuine officer on the racecourse being despatched to the grandstand. But with the race in progress few of the punters noticed anything out of the ordinary as dozens of real policemen swooped on the actors and arrested the lot. They, the fake policemen and the 'villain' with his fake gun, were all unceremoniously bundled into a police van and carted off to the police station where some explaining had to follow. Security was almost breached, filming was thus interrupted, the television company received an almighty rocket from the chief superintendent in charge of the race meeting, and Her Majesty continued to watch the horses with her normal deep interest.

I am sure her own security officers would later tell her about the incident, and knowing that she has a wonderful sense of humour, I feel sure this is one queen who would be amused.

The rapidly increasing popularity of television in the 1960s, particularly with fast-moving dramas often shown live whilst being filmed in genuine towns and villages, caused a lot of confusion in the minds of some viewers.

Because the scenes were often very realistic and set in recognizable places, some viewers believed they were real events even if they were screened in black and white. Even today, some viewers think that drama serials (i.e. soaps) are stories of real people and I have met a police officer who thought the early episodes of my series *Heartbeat* were from a police documentary.

I recall one incident in Scarborough when a gentleman rang the police in something of a panic to tell them a robbery was taking place at a building society premises directly opposite his house. He said he was actually witnessing the attack and gave a full description of the premises, the villains and their parked get-away vehicle. When the police arrived, there was no sign of any raid so they went to ask the informant a few more questions. During their interview, it transpired he was an elderly gentleman who had been watching a fictionalized crime drama on his television set. The premises attacked in the film were almost identical to the one opposite his house and so he believed he was truly witnessing a serious crime. And he had watched it in black and white!

When interviewing witnesses, police officers are always alert to the possibility that they might have been influenced by external factors, consequently it is sometimes difficult, if not impossible, to get a coherent story from the eyewitness account of just one person. The more witnesses there are to a crime, accident or other incident, the easier it is to reach the truth but even so, it is amazing just how many variations of a single simple incident can be provided by witnesses.

Even basic things like the colour or make of a motor car can vary – I once interviewed three witnesses to a hit-and-run traffic accident with one saying the offending car was dark grey, another saying it was blue and the third swearing it was dark green. Even factual evidence like the registration numbers of offending cars can be mistaken: figure 8 can be misinterpreted as letter B; letter H can be mistaken for letter A, letters M and N are often confused and even Y can be misread as J.

It was with this kind of uncertainty in mind that I found myself interviewing a rather elderly gentleman in Strensford Police Station. I was catching up with some paperwork in the inquiry office at four o'clock one Friday afternoon when he arrived in a state of great agitation. For some reason, he had chosen not to telephone, probably preferring a face-to-face interview with a police officer due to the trauma he had experienced. In fact, I discovered he lived only a couple of streets away, and so it was almost as quick to visit the police station, particularly if the line was engaged.

'Yes, sir, how can I help you?' I went to the inquiry hatch and noticed he was about seventy years old with thin grey hair, brown eyes behind dark-rimmed spectacles and a heavy moustache, also grey but stained with pipe smoke. He was a short man, only about 5' 6" tall, and he wore a rather dingy brown raincoat, although I did notice he was wearing a collar and tie.

'Er, I'm not sure.' He sounded rather nervous about this encounter. 'It's just that I saw something and thought it might be someone committing a crime. I thought I ought to report it.'

'Certainly, when did it happen?'

'Not long ago, half-an-hour perhaps, out on the moor. Twenty minutes even. I was driving my car across the moor, I'd been to visit my daughter you see, and I saw two men hitting another one outside a house, really savage they were, and then they bundled him inside and they all went in and closed the door.'

'You've not reported it earlier?'

'No, I looked for a kiosk to ring 999 but there are none. So I went home, parked the car and came straight here.'

'And where do you live?' I was now jotting down details of this report on a scrap pad and would take action once I was more sure of what the fellow had witnessed.

'Just behind the police station. Flint Street, number 22.'

'And your name, sir?'

'Campbell, Geoffrey.'

'Right, thanks. Now I need to go over this very carefully before deciding what to do. What do you think was happening? Was it someone helping a sick or injured person? A drunk? Or was it raiders attacking a householder? Young lads doing nothing more serious than messing about? Can you throw a little more light on it? And where was it? And what time was it all going on?'

By gently questioning Mr Campbell, I established that he had left his daughter's house at Thornthwaite shortly after 3.15 to drive home, and he had taken his usual route which was a minor road from Thornthwaite, heading towards the coast.

It led through Dorsley and Newbiggin before entering Strensford near the railway station, but along its route lay several isolated farmsteads and lonely cottages. Mr Campbell then assured me he had left Dorsley but not arrived at Newbiggin when he had noticed the incident, and it was at a large farmhouse on the right-hand side of the road as he was travelling along it. There was only one such house – Greystones Farm – and it was visible from the road.

Because he had been driving his car at the time, he had caught only a very short glimpse of the incident and so his account had to be treated with some scepticism, although we could not ignore it. He was sure what he had seen – two men attacking a third and bundling him into the house. In his opinion, the victim was struggling and fighting but he was overwhelmed by the others. He was unable to provide a description of any of the men, other than to say they all looked about thirty years old, had dark long hair and were wearing farm clothes. Once they had forcibly thrust the man indoors, they slammed the door — and it had all happened as Mr Campbell was driving past.

The incident had troubled him as he drove towards town, being uncertain about returning to try and find out what had been going on, and, as he told me, there were no telephone kiosks along his route after that point and so he had driven home, parked and then walked the few yards to make his report. I assured him he had done the right thing – if those men were attacking someone, Mr Campbell could have put himself in danger.

The question now was whether he escorted a police officer to the farm to ensure the correct location was checked, or whether that might place him in further danger if the villains were still on the premises and later tried to trace him. It was time for a discussion with the duty sergeant, in this case a newcomer to Strensford, Sergeant Mason. I tapped on the sergeant's office door and Mason, a pleasant fair-haired man of about thirty-five, invited us both to enter.

With Mr Campbell at my side, I repeated his story whereupon Sergeant Mason asked him a few more questions before saying, 'Nick, I think you should go out and investigate this one. Take a car with a radio, pick up PC Black in the town centre for support, and maintain radio contact. Don't take risks – go up to the farm, make a discreet recce, send me a situation report as soon as you can and we'll take it from there. I am aware that there is an allegation of violence but that no firearms or other weapons were observed. I think you, Mr Campbell, should return home, and we will let you know the outcome of this just as soon as we know what's been happening. Is that all right by you?'

'Yes, yes, of course.' And Mr Campbell sounded relieved that he had fulfilled his civic duty and that the police were heeding his story by taking positive action. He left straight away, by now much calmer and happier.

'Be careful, Nick. I'll ring Black on his

point and warn him to expect you, then go and see what this is all about. It could be nothing, farm lads larking about, brothers having a family dust-up or something similar, but we've got to investigate.'

'Right, Sarge.'

'I'll look after the office. I have some urgent paperwork to catch up on and you can keep in touch over the radio.'

I knew the road in question and so I drove into the town centre, collected Ian Black who was a young officer with about three years service, and headed out of town towards Newbiggin. En route, I explained to Black what had happened and he said he was keen to be involved; this kind of thing was infinitely better than plodding the streets for eight hours a day. As we approached Newbiggin with a sense of urgency laced with care, there was a shock. The road was closed. Massive red barriers and 'Road Closed' signs prevented any kind of access and diversion indicators were in place with a notice apologizing for the closure but informing travellers that a new replacement water main was being installed. When I checked the map in the police car I saw that Greystones Farm was about quarter of a mile beyond that barrier, and so I suggested we walk. PC Black agreed. It would take only a few minutes and although it meant temporarily being out of radio contact with Sergeant Mason, we could see no alternative. I radioed Control at Strensford to inform Sergeant Mason of our whereabouts and decision, saying we would contact him upon our return. He warned us not to take undue risks, but to ensure we did a good job. If something did happen to us, he would know where to send reinforcements.

I wondered why Mr Campbell had not mentioned this diversion because it was clearly one which had been in place for some time, even if there were no workmen present. They would have finished work at 4.30, but they had left some heavy equipment behind.

With PC Black at my side, I ducked beneath the red barrier and strode along the wide grass verge, well away from the ditch being dug down the centre of the lane to accommodate the replacement pipeline, and soon Greystones Farm came into view. We were partially sheltered by a hawthorn hedge but during our approach we had a clear view of the house and the surrounding fields and buildings. There was no doubt it looked deserted – the exterior was a mass of abandoned farm vehicles ranging from horse-drawn carts to old tractors and harvesters. Several doors of outbuildings were hanging off their hinges with windows and tiles missing, while the house itself wore an air of dereliction and neglect. I did notice, however, that there were no motor vehicles outside the farm, not even any rusting wrecks.

'It looks empty.' I muttered to Ian Black. 'And this road closure extends beyond the entrance gate. It all seems a bit odd to me.'

I told him again what Mr Campbell had seen but we had to continue to the farm gate and walk down the track which led to the house, a distance of about three hundred yards with no shelter. The track crossed open fields but, as we'd had no report of firearms or other weapons, we did not feel particularly at risk. Putting on a brave face, therefore, we marched resolutely towards the farmhouse with each step reinforcing the emptiness of all the buildings. As we approached, it was evident it had been deserted for years although that was no guarantee it had not been used for underhand or secretive purposes in spite of its condition. The front door was hanging off its hinges, most of the ground-floor windows had broken panes with grass and weeds growing between the flagstones.

Weeds also grew from the steps at the front door, and spilled over the gutters beneath the roof with more weeds sprouting from the tiles. Beyond all doubt, the place was a wreck – but it might conceal a fugitive or even a victim of crime. That was what we were seeking. As we arrived at the front door, there was no sign of activity save for a few pigeons fluttering out of the windows. Should we therefore split with one of us going to the back door and the other remaining at the front, or should we enter together in a show of strength, just in case our progress was being observed?

In the belief that our approach along that open track could have been noticed long before we reached the front door, we entered together, shouting 'POLICE' as a warning. But other than scattering more pigeons in the kitchen, it produced no reaction. No one made a dash for freedom. As we began our tour, we saw there was no furniture in the house, the floors were bare and wallpaper was hanging off the walls. The whole place smelt of dampness and neglect. Shouting again to announce our presence, and noting there were no sounds of anyone moving about, we decided to make a room-by-room search. We discovered the entire place was deserted – we checked in all the big cupboards, the bedrooms, the attic and even the cellar but there was no sign of recent occupancy. Sometimes in derelict houses, there are signs of campers, such as fires and discarded rubbish, or children may have been playing, but in this case, there was nothing. It was too far off the beaten track for children to use as a playground, and well away from any of the public footpaths.

We knew that if anyone had been inside when we arrived, we should have heard them running or walking on the bare floorboards. Satisfied that the house was deserted, we did a similar exercise in all the outbuildings. It took quite a long time, but we found nothing. No injured person, no dead body, no cache of stolen property or hidden treasure, no evidence of any crime, no illicit distillery and no sign of recent occupancy. And, of course, the lane closure extended beyond the farm gate, so what had Mr Campbell seen, and where had he seen it? Indeed, how had he seen it? He couldn't have driven past this farm. Certainly, whatever he had witnessed, did not appear to have occurred at this location. Satisfied with our search, we returned to the car and radioed Control to report that we were safe, but with a negative result. Sergeant Mason instructed us to return to Strensford, and suggested I revisit Mr Campbell to acquaint him with the result of our endeavours. Meanwhile, PC Black would resume his patrolling.

When I knocked on the door of Mr Campbell's terrace house, a woman answered. She was in her sixties, a small person with grey hair and a very fresh complexion complemented by a charming smile.

'Yes?'

'I'm PC Rhea. I'm looking for Mr Campbell,' I told her.

'He's just popped into town to get his *Evening Gazette*. He won't be long. Can I help?' There was a slight look of concern on her face; the unexpected arrival of a uniformed constable at one's door usually had that effect.

I began to explain but she invited me inside and led me into a cosy small lounge with a coal fire burning. On a side table there was a teapot, cups and biscuits and she told me Geoffrey always liked a cup of tea when he returned from getting his evening paper. He would then sit and read it while enjoying his tea.

'Would you like a cup while you're

waiting?' she invited.

I accepted and we settled down in arm-chairs beside the fire, and I turned again to the reason for my presence. I told her what Geoffrey had witnessed, with the location and time, and as my story developed, I could see her frowning.

'Oh, but he couldn't have seen that,' she interrupted me. 'He's never been out of the house today, except for a short walk earlier this afternoon. Most certainly he has not been out in his car and he has not been to visit Susan, that's our daughter. In fact, just before he went for his walk, he was asleep in that chair where you are. Lunch has that effect on him, you know, his age and all that, so when he woke up he told me he was going out for some fresh air. I had no idea he'd been to the police station.'

When I checked the times of his alleged report with her story, there was no doubt he had been at home during the material time; he could not have been driving past Greystones Farm at the time he had stated and besides, the road was blocked. It was then that I wondered if he had seen something on television which he had believed to be real. I knew this sort of thing happened with elderly people, but when

Mrs Campbell and I checked the news-papers for television programmes, we found there had been nothing on TV which might have produced this result.

'It must have been one of his dreams,' she sighed.

'Dream?'

'He's done this before, had a dream while sleeping in his chair, and then woken up to think it was real. He once thought he'd seen a man fall off the pier and get rescued, and on another occasion he thought a ship was sinking out at sea and rang the coastguard. This is by no means the first time this has happened, Mr Rhea.'

I talked through some of his dreams and it became evident this was yet another of those occasions. I decided it would be best not to worry Mr Campbell by suggesting he was causing us unnecessary work or that he might be suffering from some kind of mental problem, and so I got up to leave before he returned.

'When he comes back, Mrs Campbell, I think you should just say that the police called to say they had searched Greystones Farm, but there was no sign of an injured person. And thank him for his public-spiritedness, saying we think it was just some local lads playing around.'

'All right, I know he worries when one of his experiences turns out to be nothing but a dream, but he means no harm.'

'I know. This sort of thing happens quite often,' I said, and left. I returned to the police station and informed the sergeant, then told PC Black. It had been an interesting experience, one I would remember because I felt sure it would happen again.

Six months later, the body of a murder victim was found in Greystones Farm and two men from Hull were later arrested for the crime.

CHAPTER 4

During my time at Aidensfield, one of the regular chores undertaken by police constables was the checking of registers in hotels and boarding houses. This was especially the case in seaside resorts. The legal requirement to maintain a register of guests was governed by the Aliens Orders of 1953 to 1969, and it resulted from wartime concerns that subversive foreigners might come into our country to spy upon us or commit acts of sabotage and worse. An alien was defined as a foreigner, a subject or citizen of a foreign country

In passing a law to cater for unwelcome foreigners, however, it also included those who were perfectly law-abiding and welcome, as well as everyone else living in Britain who used hotels and boarding houses, the exceptions being those under sixteen years of age. The result was that hotel and boarding house registers provided a very useful check on the movement of people, even if many did book in under names such as Mr and Mrs Smith, Robin Hood, Donald Duck or Sherlock Holmes.

The rules governing the registers were quite simple. They said that the keeper of any premises, furnished or unfurnished, where lodging or sleeping accommodation is provided for reward (except premises exempted by the Chief Constable such as schools, hospitals, clubs, etc) shall keep a register (open to inspection by any constable or person authorized by the Secretary of State) of all persons over sixteen staying there for one night or more. Every such person, on arrival, shall give his name and nationality. If he is an alien, he shall also give particulars of his passport or alien's registration certificate, and on departure give his next destination.

It was also stipulated that any completed register must be retained for at least twelve months and of course, all references to he, his or him included she or her. In reality most registers asked for more information than the law demanded – for example, British guests were obliged only to provide their name and nationality. There was no requirement to give any address or car registration number although most registers now routinely request that kind of information. Upon arrival, guests are simply asked to fill in the register and if there is a column for something like one's address or car number, then most of us are happy to provide it. We give such information quite voluntarily, often without wondering why.

In the 1960s, therefore, with memories of World War II still strong in the public consciousness, the police carried out regular checks of these registers, partly to ensure they were being maintained in accordance with the law but also as a means of determining whether wanted or missing persons were hiding there. This was done even though criminals were unlikely to give their real names. The same might be said of people merely wanting to get away for a bit of peace and quiet, or obtaining lodgings for other very personal reasons. And few such people would give their addresses. Aliens were more strictly supervised because they had to provide details of their passports or registration certificates, as well as their next destination.

One of the reasons for conducting these regular checks resulted from a circular received by every police station once a month – it was a list of children and young persons who were missing from home.

The list received by the North Riding of Yorkshire Constabulary included youngsters missing in an area on the eastern side of the Pennines and stretching from the Scottish border down to the River Trent. Upon receipt of the list, a police constable would be ordered to check all boarding houses and hotel registers in the town to see if any of those youngsters were staying there. Most of the runaways were girls, usually teenagers varying from about thirteen to sixteen, and we had to bear in mind that a girl could legally marry once she reached sixteen. Nonetheless, a number of sixteen, seventeen and even eighteen-year-olds did run away from home. It was fairly obvious from local inquiries that lots of them had problems within the family, often with step-fathers, their mothers' male friends or even their own brother, father and grandfather. The wicked step-father might be a symbolic figure from fairy stories and love stories, but in reality he was often very real indeed, a dark and worrying figure whose behaviour prompted vulnerable girls to run away. They ran off because there was little else they could do – if they made a complaint to draw attention to their plight, few people would believe them, especially not members of their own family. In a more open society, we know why so many girls try to find a better life by running away from the family home but in the 1960s, attempts by men to have sexual relations with young girls within the family – even their natural daughters or sisters – tended to be concealed or blatantly denied if such a suggestion was aired. The family closed ranks against prying outsiders. Even incest was rarely mentioned – what went on behind closed doors in the family home was not considered a matter for the police.

People would not talk about such dark matters, and generally blamed the teenagers for being unruly and ungrateful when in fact they were truly unfortunate victims. Such victims of unlawful sexual activity included boys as well as girls with boys usually suffering from the attentions of scout masters, choir masters and even teachers, neighbours and family friends.

If these tormented youngsters did run away with a few stolen pounds in their pockets, they would often try to obtain food and rest in cheap boarding houses and, being unfamiliar with the law on registering their arrival, would cheerfully and fully complete the register, including their addresses. Few runaways tried to disguise themselves; they thought that catching a bus to a place thirty or forty miles away would provide anonymity at a sufficient and safe distance from home. Quite a large number headed for places they knew fairly well, such as resorts where they had spent a holiday or outing, either with the family or with their school. In addition, of course, there is a theory that, secretly, a lot of runaways wished to be found so that their private misery might be brought to a close when they were traced by the authorities.

It was against this background that Sergeant Mason asked me to remain behind after a morning briefing. When my colleagues had disappeared to go about their beat duties, he explained he had a special task which might require the skills of a constable more experienced than the youngsters currently patrolling the town.

He gave me the latest list of missing young persons and said, 'Nick, every quarter we check all the registers in these establishments,' and he handed me a file containing a list of all known hotels and boarding houses in Strensford. 'It's really an exercise to ensure they're keeping proper records rather than checking the names of residents. But we usually double-up the exercise at the same time by checking for a few names, probably at random, to see whether any of these missing kids are hiding there. You never know what might turn up.'

I looked at the printed list he had given me. It was a single foolscap sheet of paper printed on both sides with brief details of several youngsters who were missing from their homes in the north-east of England. In some cases, the descriptions included black-and-white photographs reprinted from family snapshots. In this case, all the youngsters were under twenty-one, most being under sixteen, and the procedure was that an adult, i.e. someone of twenty-one and over, could go missing whenever they wished without police interference. An adult has the right to leave home even if they are married with the responsibility of a family. The police would only become involved if the missing adult was suspected of crime, or was a possible victim of crime, or there was some other factor which produced serious official concern – for example, mental illness. For juveniles, it was a different matter. If a child or young person was reported missing, action to trace them was always taken by the police as a matter of priority, and if they were thought to be in real danger, then a large-scale, intensive search would be launched. Police dogs and skilled search teams, such as the mountain rescue service, might be employed if justified by the circumstances.

If youngsters merely ran away from home because of some form of romantic interlude or because of some domestic strife or a personal problem, then their names would be included in a 'Missing Persons' register, and details would be circulated to all neighbouring police forces, and to local police stations. This monthly digest was just one part of the ongoing search but it meant the police of Strensford could check all those monthly names against registers in local hotels and boarding houses.

We realized, of course, that it was highly unlikely a youngster on the run would book into an expensive or smart hotel but it was quite probable that some would take refuge in cheap boarding houses and lodgings of the kind where no questions were asked. Unless they had friends or trusted family members in the vicinity, there was nowhere else to go – except perhaps seats in bus shelters and parks, or derelict buildings. In some cases where the landladies were suspicious of a youngster booking in while alone – or perhaps with another youngster of the opposite sex or even one of the same sex – they would contact the police so that the necessary checks could be made, but some boarding house owners, perhaps with personal reasons for not wishing to involve the constabulary, kept quiet about their rather mysterious young guests. They might tell the police if the kids couldn't pay or tried to steal something, but it was amazing how many failed to report the presence of very young and vulnerable children.

It is perhaps prudent at this point to recall that many youngsters wishing to get married against parental wishes, would run away with their lover.

Some might only want a romantic week-end together in a seaside resort or quiet country inn, but those who wanted to marry in defiance of their family often headed for Gretna Green in Scotland. In the past, if the pair were over sixteen, they could be married by the village blacksmith at his anvil in Gretna even without the consent of parents or guardians. In England, a person under twenty-one years of age could not marry without the consent of their parents and so, if this permission was not granted, some determined youngsters would flee to Gretna Green whose reputation for marrying runaways started in 1754.

Even though such clandestine marriages were forbidden in England, Scottish law allowed them. All that was required from the couple was that both were over the age of sixteen, along with a declaration before witnesses of their willingness to marry. Once that was given, the ceremony could be carried out by the blacksmith of Gretna Hall at his anvil, or even the toll-keeper, the ferryman or indeed anyone else. By 1826, as many as two hundred couples were getting married at Gretna each year but after 1856 Scottish law was altered to say that at least one member of the couple must be resident in Scotland for at least twenty-one days before the marriage. This reduced numbers but lots of young English lovers who had been denied parental consent continued to head for Gretna to be married, usually by the smithy at his anvil. It follows that a lot of requests were made to the police of Dumfries and Galloway by concerned parents for searches to be made of local lodgings where youngsters from England, girls in particular, might be hiding for the necessary three weeks in preparation for their wedding.

Others might have got jobs in the area while completing the necessary residential qualification. A lot of worried fathers also went to Gretna in search of their wayward daughters. In 1940, the law was changed to prevent the blacksmith carrying out these weddings, although frustrated youngsters continued to head for Gretna for some years afterwards, mistakenly believing the custom prevailed. Marriages continued to be conducted there, albeit now by the local registrar. With the romance of Gretna having evaporated to be replaced by a solemn official, a lot of would-be brides and grooms ran off anyway. Quite often they found themselves living in cheap lodging houses in England as they tried to sort out their future.

Even so, those wanting to marry at Gretna could – and still can – do so even if the rules have changed somewhat.

The fact was, however, that quite a number of teenage runaways did not wish to get married, but instead wanted only a romantic weekend together to work out their future, unless, of course, they were running away from something or someone. Not surprisingly, many arrived in holiday resorts like Scarborough, Bridlington, Whitby and Strensford.

Armed with my file of hotels and lodging houses, plus my list of missing youngsters, therefore, I headed into town. The hotels and lodging houses were listed both in alphabetical order and street-by-street, so it was a fairly simple matter to plan a course which allowed me to visit as many as possible within a single tour of duty

There were too many to visit during a single shift, so I checked the list to see whether any youngsters were specially mentioned as being likely to head for Strensford but only one was. I could concentrate upon him but it meant looking at the list of other names and trying to memorize as many as possible so that I could speedily check the registers. Then there were a few photographs to examine and hopefully memorize. The young man who had caught my interest was aged fifteen and he had been missing for two weeks with his parents thinking he might be in Strensford. They considered this likely because it was the long-standing venue of the family's annual holiday – or had been until the lad was twelve. Apparently, once he had reached twelve, he'd expressed a desire to go to Blackpool and see the famous lights and so Blackpool Police had also been alerted to his current absence. He had not been found in Blackpool either. Since his disappearance, the family had travelled several times to Strensford and Blackpool to search for him, without success.

The family, called Chivers, all lived in Stockton-on-Tees, and for years had come to Strensford for their long summer break. The missing youngster, Duncan, would know his way around the town and his flight there had been made easier because there were good train and bus services between Stockton and Strensford. He would not need to cycle there, or to thumb lifts in passing cars. The description of Duncan stressed that even though he was only fifteen, he looked seventeen, being tall, dark and well built with a smart and confident appearance. He behaved as if he was older than his years too, and because he had worked at weekends, sometimes in a papershop and sometimes washing up in a cafe, he had saved quite a lot of money.

His parents thought he would be able to pay for his keep in lodgings, at least for a week or two, and then he was quite capable of finding a small job to pay his way. When I studied his description, it ended with the sentence, 'May be in the company of Stephanie Lewis aged fifteen, also reported missing from home. See entry NRC 334/66.' This episode therefore looked like a young couple wanting a romantic tryst even if both were under age. A modern Romeo and Juliet. I read Stephanie's description and saw she was a small blonde girl, very pretty and charming, and she also hailed from Stockton.

There was no suggestion in either report that these kids were at risk or in danger of any kind, nor were they suspected of committing any criminal offence. They were just a couple of young lovers who had apparently run away to be together without any hint of marriage, one of many in a similar predicament throughout history. But surely, if they were in one of our local lodging houses, their presence would raise a query in the minds of either the landlady or the other guests? Even if Duncan looked older than fifteen, Stephanie did look her age according to the report. But I knew that girls could skilfully use make-up and clothes to make themselves appear older. It was quite feasible the couple could pass themselves off as a young married couple.

My tour of boarding establishments quickly settled into a routine examination of dozens of registers. I soon realized that most had been produced by the same local printer because the layout of the pages in most registers was identical which made my work a little easier.

In addition to asking for a guest's name and nationality, there were columns for their date of arrival, address, car number, telephone number, date of departure and even comments about the establishment, especially its comfort and the food. Most of the smaller establishments had a side table in the entrance hall and the register lay open upon that, with no one in attendance, making it easy for me to undertake my task. In the larger hotels, it lay open on the counter of the reception office, generally with a receptionist hovering nearby.

I found most of the landladies and

landlords were very helpful, and that all kept their registers in accordance with the regulations. And, of course, they were accustomed to regular police checks of this kind. Some offered me tea or coffee which provided an opportunity to ask if any youngsters had tried or succeeded in securing accommodation, but none had. As the day wore on with dozens of establishments visited, it looked as if my quest was going to be unproductive. And then I spotted the name of Duncan Chivers in a register. The entry was for Mr and Mrs Duncan Chivers and it included an address at Stockton-on-Tees. I felt a quickening of my pulse as I realized I had surely found one or probably two of the missing youngsters, masquerading as Mr and Mrs. The place was a boarding house called Ocean View which was a five storey house in a sweeping arcade; it was a very smart establishment with a clean frontage and a handkerchief-sized front lawn which was neatly trimmed with rose bushes around it. From my position in the entrance hall, I could see that the dining-room and lounge looked extremely comfortable and well equipped.

I thought it was hardly the sort of place a young man of fifteen would take his girl –

unless he was rather sophisticated and had money to spend. Perhaps Duncan had such assets? Nothing surprises an experienced police officer.

Now it was time to quiz the landlady and my file said her name was Mrs Cynthia Stubbins. In deciding to ask her a few questions, I realized I must be careful not to scare away the youngsters, or to be precise, not to let her scare them away. I needed to establish they were still living here because the register entry did not state how long they intended staying, and then I must decide how to deal with them, perhaps even asking Stockton Police to visit their parents to persuade them to come and collect the runaways from either this boarding house or the police station. A car journey from Stockton to Strensford would take at least an hour, and then there was the time lapse in getting organized for the trip. It was now almost three o'clock in the afternoon.

However, my first task was to establish they were still resident and I spotted a bell which said, 'Ring for attention'. I pressed it and a large dark-haired woman appeared from behind a curtain. She would be in her late fifties, I estimated, smartly dressed with an air of efficiency.

'Yes?' she asked, frowning at the sight of a constable in uniform.

'Mrs Stubbins?'

'Yes.'

'PC Rhea, I'm making the quarterly check of hotel and boarding house registers. I've inspected yours, all seems to be in order.'

'I make sure it is, constable. It is always open for inspection, as I am sure you have noted.'

'Thank you for that. However, there is one question I would like to ask: I notice you have a Mr and Mrs Duncan Chivers staying here. Are they here now, on the premises, by any chance?'

'No, I do not allow my lodgers to be on the premises during the day, constable, this is a bed-and-breakfast establishment. They sleep here, have their breakfast and then go out for the day. They return in the early evening, usually around four or five o'clock, perhaps have a cup of tea which I can supply, and then get changed before going into town for a meal or a show. They all do that. Mr and Mrs Chivers will be somewhere in town, constable, or perhaps on the beach, and I expect them back around teatime. They usually return fairly early, about four o'clock for a cup of tea and a scone, and then go to their room. That has been their practice so far.'

'How long are they staying?'

'Until the weekend, they will leave on Saturday morning after breakfast.'

It was Tuesday now and so I had plenty of time to track them down, but I realized that if Mrs Stubbins warned them I had been asking after them, they would promptly leave and disappear once again. Runaways did that sort of thing if they sensed they were about to be traced. I had to be very careful how I approached the problem of questioning Mrs Stubbins any further, preferably giving the impression that the couple were not escaped convicts or dangerous criminals wanted for some serious offence. I did not want her to eject them from the premises!

I wanted them to remain until I had clarified the whole matter. For one thing, I had to be sure this Mr and Mrs Chivers was in fact the young couple I was seeking.

'Can I give them a message?' she asked as I pondered my next course of action.

'No thanks, it's not serious, it's a personal matter. I'm on duty all day, so I'll try to return about 4.30 and hope to catch them then. Please don't tell them I have been ask-ing about them, I would prefer to talk to them without any pre-knowledge on their part.'

'I do hope they are not criminals or wanted by the police for anything, this is a respectable establishment, constable, not one of those cheap and nasty places. I am very particular who I accept as guests in my house.'

'They're not wanted for any crime, Mrs Stubbins, I can assure you of that. I would just like a private chat with them.'

'Oh, well, I suppose it's nothing to do with me. But yes, if you call back later, you might catch them before they go into town for the evening.'

As I left, I felt I had dealt diplomatically with this so far, although I did ponder the wisdom of calling Stockton Police immediately, with a view to getting the parents prepared to make the trip to collect their offspring. The sooner I got them moving, the more likely it was that the pair would be returned to the care of their families. The only worry niggling away at the back of my mind was that this boarding house was not the sort of place to be frequented by a couple of runaway children, it was far too classy.

Furthermore, I got the impression that Mrs Stubbins was not the sort of landlady who would tolerate a runaway couple of children on her premises, and certainly she wouldn't allow them to share a bedroom. She'd realize immediately they were too young to be married. It meant I must set eyes on the pair and get them positively identified before I did anything else.

Sergeant Mason met me at one of my conference points and so I informed him of my progress. Although I had visited lots of other hotels and boarding houses, I had not found any trace of runaways and, after discussing the Chivers case together with my own uncertainties, he agreed with my course of action.

'Get them identified, Nick, and if it's them, put them in the car and bring them to the police station. That's the procedure, get them into a place of safety – and a police station qualifies as that! Then we can ring Stockton and get the parents to collect them, although the lad will have to be quizzed to see if he has committed any offence against the girl. And she against him! I'll make sure we have a policewoman available if the girl is brought in. Don't forget, they're both under the age of consent although they are both fifteen, and we don't necessarily want to prosecute youngsters of that age for what one of our learned judges described as enjoying a tumble in the hay!'

And so it was that I returned to Ocean View just after four o'clock. There was no sign of anyone in the dining-room having tea and the entrance hall was deserted, so I rang the bell as before. Once again, Mrs Stubbins materialized from behind the large curtain.

'Ah, PC Rhea, Mr and Mrs Chivers are in their room. They have ordered tea so shall you join them? They will take it in the dining-room, that door to your right.'

'Will the room be empty otherwise?' I did not want other tea-drinkers to listen to our conversation.

'Yes, none of my other guests have returned for tea. If they do, I shall inform you.'

'All right, I'll join the Chivers for tea, it will make things very civilized,' and so she led me into the dining-room where a table was set. There was a two-tier plate of cakes in the middle, plus a hot teapot, sugar, milk, cup and saucers, and it all made me wonder how a lad of fifteen had seen fit to bring his youthful lover to this kind of place. She went upstairs to summon the happy couple and I waited with, admittedly, some apprehension.

A few minutes later the door opened and Mrs Stubbins popped her head around it and said, 'PC Rhea, Mr and Mrs Chivers.'

In walked a man and woman who must each have been at least sixty years old. They looked highly surprised and somewhat embarrassed to find a policeman awaiting them. But they weren't as surprised as me. Mrs Stubbins made a discreet exit and closed the door. I stood up, waved my hands to indicate they should join me for tea, and then wondered how I was going to talk my way out of this.

'Did they tell you?' Mrs Chivers demanded before sitting down. She looked highly embarrassed at thus confrontation. 'The family? Did they report us and get you to come looking for us? Like criminals?'

'Erm, no,' I said. 'Look, please sit down and have some tea. I am not looking for you, I am looking for a pair of teenagers who have run away. I was expecting a pair of fifteen-year-olds to appear, not you. The name's the same, you see, the young man is Duncan Chivers but his girl is also from Stockton-on-Tees, so when I read the entry in the register...'

'Well, someone must have been onto you, getting you to check on us like this, this is very embarrassing, people should mind their own business.' Mrs Chivers was clearly not going to let this embarrassing matter rest and appeared not to have heeded or understood my apology. I got the impression she wasn't listening to a word I said. 'Folks are always poking their noses into other folks' business...'

However, Mr Chivers, a calm, round-faced man with a slightly florid complexion beneath his grey hair, settled down and bade his wife to be quiet for just a moment. She sat down, flustered and upset, but neither of them bothered with the teapot. I felt something of a Charley, sitting at a tea-table in my uniform on what was supposed to be an inquiry of some delicacy.

'Tell me again, constable, just why are you here?' he asked. 'I missed what you said...'

'A pair of fifteen-year-olds from Stockton have run away from home,' I told him. 'A boy and a girl. Their families think they might have come here, to Strensford, so I have been touring all the boarding houses and hotels, checking their registers to see if the kids have booked in. They are called Duncan Chivers and Stephanie Lewis. So when I saw your names, Mr and Mrs Duncan Chivers, in Ocean View's register, along with the Stockton address, I thought it was them, sharing a room. I was duty bound to make the necessary inquiries...'

Mrs Chivers looked at me and demanded, 'Silly children! Why do they do such things? So our families didn't ask you to look for me and Duncan? They're not behind this?'

'No, not at all. I am not looking for you. As I said, I'm looking for two teenagers, these two,' and I produced the sheet of 'Missing From Home' juveniles and showed it to them, as if to justify my story.

'That's my name,' said Mrs Chivers. 'I am called Stephanie Lewis, and if it's of any interest to you, I'm that Stephanie's grand-mother.'

'And I am Duncan's grandfather. We have run away, PC Rhea, our respective families did not approve of our relationship, so we've run away to Strensford, pretending to be man and wife. Mr and Mrs Chivers.'

'Ah.' I could now see the reason for their initial embarrassment.

'The landlady does not know we are not married, I think she might have refused us if she had known,' smiled Mr Chivers. 'This is between you and us, of course, I trust it will go no further but I think you need an ex-planation.'

'Thanks.' This part of the inquiry was now much clearer, even if I had not found the youngsters. 'I'm sorry to have put you through this.'

'It's not your fault, Constable, we are to blame but we came away for a bit of peace and quiet while we made a decision about our own future. So I wonder if young Duncan and Stephanie have done the same?'

I didn't know how to react. Instead of finding two children, I had unwittingly uncovered their grandparents' plot. In response, I picked up the teapot and poured them each a cup, saying, 'I think we all need a cup of tea after this.'

'I think we do,' said 'Mrs' Chivers.

As we sat and enjoyed the tea, they told me about their late-life romance, two bereaved grandparents who had found love against joint family expectations and wishes, and so they had literally run away to be alone, pretending to be man and wife. And I had disturbed their happy love-nest – but I tended to agree that the children might have emulated them.

'Have they looked in Blackpool for Duncan?' suggested his grandfather. 'He once told me that's where he would go.'

'Stephanie was the same,' said her granny. 'She adores Blackpool.'

'Yes,' I told them. 'The police over there

have been alerted but I understand no trace of them has been found.'

We sat for half-an-hour or so, drinking tea and discussing family problems until, in the end, we were laughing and joking about it all. 'Mrs Chivers' was now relaxed and laughing at their predicament. I promised not to reveal their whereabouts but I knew I must inform Mrs Stubbins of the real reason for my visit. I had to kill any rumours that might be generated by my presence. I told Duncan and Stephanie of my intention, which was to save them from further embarrassment. And I said I would ring Stockton Police to suggest they asked Blackpool Police to carry out yet another of their many searches for two missing teenagers.

Then I went to the dining-room door and called in Mrs Stubbins. She had not been listening at the keyhole because she was in her kitchen.

'I thought I ought to explain,' I said to her. 'I am looking for two missing teenagers, Duncan Chivers and Stephanie Lewis who are both fifteen. When I saw this gentleman's name in your register, sharing a room, I thought it was those youngsters. Now I know it wasn't them! We all thought you ought to know, and we did enjoy the tea!'

'I would never allow two children of that age to share a room in this establishment, PC Rhea. I can spot a runaway romantic a mile off! But now you mention it, a couple of that age did try to get in here only last weekend, but I sent them packing. I told them to try Seacrest, that's more in their line.'

'Seacrest?' I checked my list and discovered I had not yet visited it. 'I'll check there before I knock off duty.'

'And if you find them, call their parents, not us!' laughed Duncan Chivers.

Mrs Stubbins did not appreciate his joke but when I called at Seacrest, young Duncan Chivers and Stephanie Lewis were there, preparing for an evening in town. I had to spoil their night out by taking them to the police station and calling their parents, but I never told any of them that Duncan's grandad and Stephanie's grandmother were staying only a few doors away, having also run away from home. In some was, it was surprising they had not encountered one another in town, but Strensford is a busy place in spite of its size and, of course, the haunts of teenagers vary considerably from those of a more senior age.

It later transpired that the youngsters had decided to run away because their grandparents had done so. 'What's good for them is good for us,' said young Duncan.

One of the unsettling facts about boarding house registers, and probably hotel registers to a lesser degree, was that they were usually kept open on a table or counter near an entrance to which some members of the public had access. Anyone visiting a boarding house, perhaps to enquire about vacancies or even to make a delivery of some kind, could, while awaiting attention, read (and make a record of) details of the recently entered names and addresses. In hotels, the register was usually supervised by the receptionist and so its contents were not quite so vulnerable. The same might be said of visitors' books in places like museums, art galleries, churches, exhibitions of various kinds or even show houses – quite often, the books would contain columns asking for a visitor's name, address and comments; sensible visitors did not enter their full address, but merely gave the town or even the county from which they had come. In this way they contributed to the success of the venture in question while retaining some of their privacy.

The danger of providing one's complete address in such a book is obvious – it tells a potential burglar, housebreaker or thief that you are away from home, probably for an extended period. This was particularly the case in seaside boarding houses where a column asked for the departure date of the guest, or even their next destination and some would cheerfully and innocently complete the entry.

Thus a criminal might know that you were away for a week or more, or heading off to the Lake District or Scotland following a trip to Strensford. And if you were away for that length of time, your empty house was an easy target for a determined and crafty villain. I know of no statistics which seek to highlight or analyse this problem but as police officers, we made regular efforts to alert boarding house keepers and hotel receptionists to these dangers. Some promised to take more care with their registers; others told us to mind our own business, their belief being they did not have to be told by a lowly constable how to run their business. To be honest, the number of cases where housebreakers and their ilk had made use of such knowledge was unknown – there was no way the constabularies' crime figures or Home Office statistics would produce this kind of information.

In spite of that, I found myself dealing with such a case in Strensford. I ought to add that in detecting some crimes, a good deal of luck is often required, or even a coincidence or two and this could be especially the case if the crime was committed out of one's own force area.

It happened like this. Each day prior to starting their eight-hour patrol of Strensford, the town's constables would parade for duty in the muster room ten minutes before their shifts began. They would be inspected by the sergeant to ensure they were smartly dressed and had their 'appointments', i.e. their truncheon, whistle, handcuffs and notebook. Then they would be addressed by the sergeant who would inform them of any recent crimes in the town so that they could make general inquiries.

In addition, they would be made aware of any events which could require their attention, perhaps traffic congestion outside a church during a wedding or funeral, a parade of some kind – in fact, anything of local interest. We had also to read various circulars, such as the list of missing persons to which I have already referred. Another of those weekly circulars was issued by the West Riding Criminal Record Office: it comprised four foolscap printed pages listing the more serious unsolved crimes in No.2 District. No.2 District was a police area which included the whole of Yorkshire, Durham and Northumberland and so these weekly *Crime Informations* as they were known, contained brief details of outstanding crimes such as murder, arson, rape, burglary, housebreaking, sacrilege, frauds and serious assaults. In some cases, suspects were named, but generally there was little more than a brief description of the wanted person.

We were supposed to read all those papers, hopefully remembering at least some of the contents which might result in observations and inquiries in our own town. Whenever I undertook duty at Strensford, therefore, those *Crime Informations* were part of my regular reading. I suppose I read them in the hope that I might identify and arrest one of the wanted criminals, not a very likely outcome as most of the crimes mentioned had been committed in places like Newcastle, Middlesbrough, Leeds, Wakefield, Huddersfield, Doncaster, Sheffield or Hull. It wasn't likely that a hunted villain from such a conurbation would find his way to Strensford – but nothing was impossible.

One day I was plodding through a recent

edition of the *Crime Informations* and chanced to read about a series of house-breakings in the West Riding of Yorkshire. Widely spread around the West Riding, they had occurred during the summer months, almost invariably during daylight hours, probably around the lunchtime period, and in all cases the owners of the attacked houses had been away on holiday. For that reason, there was little or no cash in the houses, the housebreaker usually making off with saleable but easily portable valuables such as radios, small items of jewellery, ornaments in china or glass, clocks, candlesticks, cutlery and even books and small paintings. Little of his plunder was high value goods but it was all readily saleable and difficult for the owners to positively identify as theirs if they saw it for sale. If money had been left in the houses, then he would take that too, but most people rarely left money in their homes when they were on holiday. They needed every penny! One problem with housebreakings and burglaries committed when the house-holders were away on holiday, was that the crime was not discovered until some time after it had occurred, thus giving the villain time to dispose of the stolen goods. In most cases, the police were following cold trails.

On two occasions during this particular series of crimes, a car had been noticed near the attacked premises during the material times – it was described as dark coloured, perhaps a very dark blue or dark green, and probably a Ford. Witnesses could not be absolutely certain, although both witnesses, at two different locations, said the registration number was BOG 883.

The owner of BOG 883, which was a navy blue Ford Consul saloon, had been traced but eliminated from the inquiries because he had an alibi which placed him almost seventy miles away from the crime scenes at the time the offences were committed. It was therefore thought that BOG 883 was a false registration number, although it was pointed out that the figures 3 and 8 could often be mistaken or misread. It was possible that the witnesses had mistaken the number, although various combinations of those figures had been checked, and the various vehicle owners eliminated from the enquiries. It was almost certain, therefore, that the BOG 883 being used for the crimes was a false number.

The message in the *Crime Informations* was that all police officers were asked to keep observations for BOG 883 and report its whereabouts to Detective Sergeant Welburn of Wakefield CID, but not to intercept it or interview the driver. A trace of its movements was required. I read this and smiled at the number – the letters formed an unforgettable word and the figures were the last three of my seven-figure RAF National Service number. One's military number was something no serviceman ever forgot. It was an easy number for me to memorize; I would have no trouble looking for BOG 883.

Rather to my surprise, I found it soon afterwards in the register of a boarding house called Windcrest. Although it was out of the holiday season and the town was blissfully quiet, there was a shortage of manpower due to three men being away on courses, and a further three ill with flu.

I had been called in to supplement the existing manpower and was undertaking checks on boarding house registers. I came across that car number beside the name of John G. Burton who had provided a Wakefield address. It was a flat – flat 3 at an address in Portland Terrace, Wakefield. He was lodging at Windcrest for the week, having arrived on the Saturday afternoon to depart the following Saturday morning. And he was alone. Not only that, he seemed to be the only resident that week. I spotted those details in the book as it lay open in the entrance hall. However, before I could check it thoroughly the landlady, Mrs Grace Wallace, appeared and offered me a cup of tea. As it was mid-morning, and I had not managed to gain myself a drink, I accepted. It was clear she would welcome someone to talk to. She led me into her dining-room where, over tea and biscuits, we chatted about nothing in particular with me saying I would check the register after this very welcome break.

'It's a quiet time just now.' She was a pleasant woman in her mid fifties. 'The summer's over so we get a few people in, those who like a quiet time, and then we'll get busy at half-term and again as Christmas approaches. And then, once that holiday is over, we'll be virtually empty until Easter, and then it starts all over again.'

'I see you've only one guest in now.' Such a lack of guests at this time of year was not particularly unusual.

'Yes, he's Mr Burton. He's one of my regulars, comes here quite a lot, usually in the season. He's a very quiet man, PC Rhea, keeps himself to himself. He's quite young too, in his thirties, I would say, so you'd

157

think he would have a girlfriend or wife, but he hasn't anyone.'

'He's out now, I see.' I was looking down into Windcrest's empty car park to see if BOG 883 was there.

'Yes, he goes off somewhere every day, I can't do with guests in the house during the day. I have no idea where he gets to, he never says, although once or twice he has said he likes to explore the area.'

'Is he a hiker or something? A birdwatcher maybe?'

'No, nothing like that. I've never seen him in big boots and sweaters: he's usually very smart in a blazer or suit. In fact, I have no idea what his interests are, and it would be impolite to ask. He goes off alone in his car and comes back for the evening, usually eating in town, or getting fish and chips. Then he comes back before bedtime and spends most of his time in his room.'

'He must like it here!'

'Well, I think he does; he was here for a week in June, another in July and then two weeks in August. And he was here earlier in the year, just after Easter for a week. Those are my busy times.'

As we talked, a rather sinister thought crossed my mind but I did not mention it to

Mrs Wallace. Instead, I became determined to scrutinize her register to check the precise dates of Mr Burton's stays. After the tea, I returned to the register and began to check it – I found nothing unlawful or careless in the way it was maintained. I did, however, jot down the dates Mr Burton had stayed in Windcrest earlier that year noting that his car number was also included in his entries. And I checked further back too, because such registers must be retained for at least twelve months.

This one went back two years.

'You've given it a good going over!' She smiled before I left.

'I've been checking it for the names of missing youngsters: it's something we do from time to time. But thanks, it's all in good order. So are you expecting Mr Burton back this evening?'

'Oh yes, he said he would be back about five, then he'll go out for a meal somewhere.'

'Well, thanks for your time, Mrs Wallace.'

And so I left. I returned to the police station to check the *Crime Informations* for the dates of the raids in West Yorkshire, especially those where BOG 883 had been noticed. And they coincided with the dates

Mr Burton was staying at Windcrest and I began to suspect he was really the West Riding housebreaker. So did he select his victims from the register? Or from registers in other lodging houses? Had those victims come here on holiday? Had West Yorkshire police established a link between the raids and Strensford?

If Burton was the culprit, it was so easy for him to read the name and address of anyone on holiday in Windcrest, for a lot of West Riding people did come to Strensford during the summer. He could pick and choose his victims. And even if his car number matched the suspect vehicle, he could say – and prove – he was miles away at the time. He could justifiably claim it was easy for a thief to use a false car number – his number in fact. There was more to suggest he was a criminal too – he appeared to have no regular job because he spent a lot of time in Strensford, alone.

And he never talked about himself or what he did with his time. With travel by motor car very easy between the West Riding and the coast, he could come and stay here, but during the day drive back to the West Riding, commit his crimes and then return to Strensford, thus creating a false alibi, suggesting he had never left Strensford. Mrs Wallace would confirm he was staying with her. I had no idea whether he had been interviewed in depth about the raids; perhaps the fact that he openly owned BOG 883 and was in Strensford at the material times was sufficient to convince the West Riding detectives of his innocence? Or had they asked him precisely where he had been during those daytime periods when he was away from his digs? I knew he had ample time to leave Strensford after breakfast and arrive in one of the West Riding conurbations before lunch, break into a selected house or houses using addresses he had found in Strensford, and return to his digs in the early evening. And if he operated in his home patch, where his distinctive car number was known, his presence there would not be questioned either.

I decided I must convey my suspicions to someone more senior.

I asked to speak to Detective Sergeant Brewer, the senior detective in Strensford, and he listened to my theories with evident interest, particularly when the dates of Burton's presence in the town coincided with the break-ins featured in the *Crime Informations*. While I was there, he telephoned the

Criminal Record Office at the West Riding Police Headquarters and asked if John G. Burton, with an address in Wakefield, had a criminal record. He was told 'No'. That meant his fingerprints would not be on record.

Then he rang Detective Sergeant Welburn, the officer who was trying to collate sightings of BOG 883 and relayed my theories to him, expressing his own belief that there may be substance in them. He asked whether the occupants of previously attacked premises had been on holiday in Strensford at the material times, but such detail had not been recorded in the files. Welburn did say, however, that John G. Burton had himself reported a break-in at his flat whilst he was in Strensford – but I thought this was another attempt to cover up his real activities.

The result of those deliberations meant that Detective Sergeant Brewer and Detective Constable Read went up to Windcrest that evening to await the return of Burton in BOG 883. And in the boot, they found a suitcase full of property stolen that day from a house in Sandal, near Wakefield. A neighbour and keyholder had reported the break-in because the owners were on holiday in Strensford, at a boarding house called Cliff View. Clearly he visited other boarding houses to obtain target addresses. I was given the privilege of charging him with that crime and informing him that several other reported crimes would now be investigated.

And, of course, because he was now under arrest, we could take his fingerprints, search his flat and car for further evidence, and re-interview all those earlier victims. It seemed that Burton was a professional criminal, but one who had never been caught. By entering his car number in that boarding house register, he had effectively established a good alibi, but it also led to his arrest and ultimate conviction.

CHAPTER 5

Continuing the theme of seaside hotels and boarding houses, the most common offence against their proprietors was committed by people who obtained bed-and-breakfast and perhaps an evening meal, then left without paying. Some fraudsters stayed for only one night before travelling further to do the same thing in another boarding house, but others spent a week or even longer in one place before vanishing without paying the considerable bill. The proprietors of hotels and boarding houses were constantly alert to the fact this might happen but in spite of their caution, and their wise recording of car registration numbers of guests and other details, these crimes continued and a lot of fraudsters were never caught.

Some victims did not bother to inform the police, preferring to regard the debt as a matter between themselves and the crooked customer. However, if the police were notified, the crime was recorded along with a description of the accused and any details of his or her behaviour, method of transport and so forth. Details would then be circulated to all neighbouring police forces and local police stations in the hope that the culprit would be caught. Officers would then warn all boarding houses and hotels within their jurisdiction that a travelling fraudster may be operating in the locality, and they would provide his or her description in an attempt to catch the crook or prevent further crimes on their patch.

One problem with this type of fraud was that it was sometimes considered a civil matter and therefore of no concern to the police. In other words, it was not a criminal offence.

For example, if a builder did some work for a customer and the customer never paid his bill, that would not be a matter for the police. Remedies were available in the civil courts. However, if that same customer had deliberately been dishonest when commissioning the work, doing so with the intention of never paying and not having the means to pay, it might be argued he had committed a criminal offence, i.e. obtaining credit by fraud, even if his intent at the time might be difficult to prove. That offence was contained in the Debtors Act of 1869 which was still in force during the early 1960s and it catered for those who, for example, ordered and obtained a meal in a restaurant without having the means to pay for it or those with no intention of paying. It also included those who used hotels and boarding houses and left without paying, or indeed anyone who ordered goods with neither the intention nor means of paying. The Larceny Act of 1916 created a similar offence known as false pretences and this criminalized anyone who by any false pretence obtained money, chattels or valuable securities. To falsely obtain a ride in a train, for example, did not involve obtaining property it was a mere advantage and thus not covered by the Larceny Act. Thus one statute made it illegal to obtain *credit* by fraud while the other did likewise for the obtaining of *goods* by false pretences. The problem with criminal offences is that they are all a matter of words, which is why lawyers can be so entertaining in court as they argue the precise meaning of a word or phrase. Whether an action is morally wrong is not the point – it all depends upon whether the relevant words cater for the behaviour. Many a true villain has been freed due to the precise interpretation of a statute.

The truth about both these offences of fraud was that they contained legal complexities which were far too elaborate to itemize in these pages, but sadly the phraseology allowed some dishonest customers and businessmen to avoid the criminal law by becoming involved in what were euphemistically known as 'unsatisfactory business transactions', the legal term for failing to pay one's bills.

I was reminded of this whilst on duty in Strensford. One of the town's hotel owners, upon whom we periodically called to check the register and to warn of travelling fraudsters, was called Ivor Bindwood. With his wife, he owned and ran Beachview Private Hotel, a smart twenty-bedroom establishment overlooking the shoreline close to the harbour. Being a private hotel, it did not have a public bar although it had taken advantage of changes brought about by the Licensing Act of 1964. This meant that Beachview held a combined restaurant and residential licence which allowed Mr and Mrs Bindwood to sell intoxicants to their residents while enjoying a meal and there was no doubt the hotel was popular and well run. Certainly, it had a good reputation both in the town and further afield.

When I was about to embark on one of my official visits to carry out a routine inspection of the register and to alert the Bindwoods about the latest batch of travelling fraudsters, Sergeant Mason smiled rather wickedly.

'Nick,' he said. 'I see Ivor Bindwood's hotel is on your list. Beachview, a nice place. Well run. You've not met him, have you?'

'No, is there something I should know about?' And then he told me about Ivor Bindwood.

Bindwood was a retired sergeant from the London Metropolitan Police and, before joining the force, he had been a drill sergeant

167

at a military training camp. Upon retirement from the police service he had achieved his ambition, which was to buy and run a modest private hotel. With so much formal experience in other professions, it was not surprising that everything in his hotel was run on military-like lines, which he believed created and ensured efficiency. Added to this, however, was more than a dose of police influence which he believed encouraged good behaviour among his customers. For example, residents were expected to arrive for meals precisely on time; there was no smoking in the dining-room; dress at breakfast and dinner must not be too casual; guests must not enter their bedroom or even go upstairs while wearing muddy footwear; wet clothes must not be taken into the bedroom and there was a host of other similar petty rules, all highlighted on the noticeboard in reception, and in welcoming packs in every bedroom. Somewhat surprisingly, his customers seemed to enjoy this kind of rigid certainty and honesty because the hotel service was excellent, the food wonderful and the cleanliness legendary. Furthermore, the hotel's accommodation was usually fully booked on account of its reputation for being trouble-free.

The sergeant went on to say that Ivor Bindwood was widely known for trying to attract the so-called cream of society to his hotel. This had been gleaned from his former colleagues and friends who came to stay at Beachview. Lots of serving and retired police officers from his own force came to stay at Beachview and no doubt expected the best of attention from a former colleague.

Whenever policemen were on holiday they would often approach the local bobbies for a chat and to introduce themselves in the hope they could make use of the fellowship that went with 'being in the job'. These chats were usually to compare notes but also to find out where the best nightclubs were, and which pubs ignored licensing hours! From these chats, Sergeant Mason had learned that, during his police service, Bindwood had been something of a sycophant. He'd developed quite a reputation for flattering those in command, always trying to seek their praise and approbation. Not surprisingly, he was known as Creeper behind his back, some thinking this was because of his surname but others knowing it stemmed from his adulatory behaviour towards those in senior positions.

He had never risen above the rank of

sergeant because he had never passed the necessary examinations but now, in civvy street, he continued his flattery of high-ranking people by the way he pitched the advertisements for Beachview. He wanted to attract clientele such as senior military officers, senior police officers, business leaders and council officials and he worked on this ambition by advertising in their professional magazines or handing advertising leaflets to them whenever he met them socially. To make his selected VIP guests feel more welcome upon arrival, there was always a free bottle of champagne in their rooms, and if wives accompanied men, there were bouquets of flowers too. If he knew the visitors were senior police officers, i.e. superintendents or those with higher rank, he would offer generous discounts. I did not venture to suggest that this behaviour might be considered a bribe in some legal circles, although in the wider world it was regarded as good commercial practice.

Apparently Bindwood believed that by attracting society's top people as well as those with money he would secure a firm and successful future and become the owner of a hotel with a very high reputation. It all seemed to make sound business sense and so I listened with interest to Sergeant Mason's description of Bindwood's hotel and those interesting facets of his character.

'When you get there,' he continued, 'Ivor will take immense pleasure in informing you that there is no need to alert him to the likelihood of fraudsters trying to diddle him. He reckons he can spot a crook a mile off and insists that no villain will ever get the better of him. And if one did try his hand, I think Ivor would arrest him on the spot and fetch him here. He once did that with a wedding guest who merely threatened to be a trouble-maker. After a few glasses of champagne, the chap was just getting a bit stroppy and loud-mouthed when he found himself in an arm-lock before being marched, in his wedding suit, through town to the cells upon Ivor's allegation that he had been guilty of conduct likely to cause a breach of the peace.'

I thanked the sergeant for providing this useful background and so began yet another tour of boarding houses. It was eleven when I arrived at Beachview Private Hotel and wondered whether this reportedly rigid fellow would offer me a coffee or cup of tea he might be one of the old fashioned coppers for whom cups of tea were considered bribes and besides, I was a mere constable. Had I been the superintendent on an official visit, I felt sure he would prove highly co-operative, and I also wondered how he would regard my visit to check on his register.

When I arrived, I found myself in a smart reception area with a counter and a bell with a sign saying, 'Press for attention'. I did so whereupon a tall, smart man in a dark blazer and flannels emerged from an adjoining office. He was more than six feet tall with short cropped black hair cut immaculately, a black moustache equally well trimmed, black polished shoes and trousers with creases you could cut yourself upon. Certainly, the fellow had a presence and I felt like standing to attention!

'Ah, the constabulary,' he smiled warmly. 'Glad to meet you. I'm Ivor Bindwood, the owner.'

'PC Rhea,' I introduced myself, adding that I was not stationed in Strensford but was here temporarily to complement the shortage of local officers. 'I'm doing the usual check of registers but in addition,' I added, 'I wanted to warn you about a travelling fraudster who is targetting good quality private hotels, and leaving without paying.'

'PC Rhea, I did twenty-five years in the Met and I can smell a villain a mile off. You don't have to tell me about the dregs of our society. I've had more of them on charges than you've had hot dinners. If one comes here to try it on, he'll know he's met his match. But thanks anyway.'

Not to be dismissed quite so quickly, I said, 'His name is William Marshall, but he uses several aliases including Farrell, Gover, Russell, Fennimore and Read, he's got a long record for fraud of various kinds. He's thought to be moving around the north-east right now. He's forty-two, smartly dressed with blond hair and he has a strong Birmingham accent.'

'Shouldn't be too hard to spot then? But if he dares to even try to book in here, Mr Rhea, he will feel the weight of my size eleven on his backside and if he tries anything, he'll find himself in your cells before he can think of another false name.'

I smiled at his reaction and thanked him, adding, 'I have to look through your register as well, the usual check.'

'No problem, the law is the law, and I do know what you have to do. So come into the office, and how about a coffee while you're at it? The register will be in order and completely up-to-date, I can guarantee that.'

'I'm sure it will.' I followed him into a large

and airy office containing two desks one of which was clearly his. The other was not currently in use and so he indicated I should sit at that one; he produced his register and rang the kitchen for two coffees. Then, as I began to turn the pages he settled at his own desk and continued to work, not interrupting me with meaningless chatter. I was pleased about that – it's not easy running even simple checks with people talking all the time.

While I was working through entries for the past twelve months, his phone rang several times, sometimes to make room bookings, sometimes to check orders or delivery times, and sometimes to book meals in the restaurant. It was clearly a busy and popular place with the boss doing most of the admin work. Mrs Bindwood never appeared, and I guessed she looked after the domestic side of things, such as the bedrooms, laundry and cleaning.

As we worked in silence, there was a longer and more detailed telephone call, clearly of more interest to him than the earlier ones.

Although I did not deliberately listen to his end of the chatter I could not avoid overhearing some of it. It was clearly a large-scale booking for the coming April and, judging from his facial expressions, he regarded it as important.

'You want to book every room in the hotel? Yes, that shouldn't be a problem, we have fifteen doubles and five singles. If you book the entire hotel, you could use the lounge for your meeting as you suggest. The facilities will be all yours.'

I heard him ask for the required dates, which were several months ahead and he confirmed that all the rooms were available at that time; the enquiry was about a small weekend conference from the Friday evening until Sunday lunchtime in September with all meals in the hotel. There would be no official events on the Friday evening so that delegates could relax after their journey and socialize with one another. Dinner would be rather informal, taken at a time the individual guests wished – they would not arrive all together, each making their own arrangements for travel. On the Saturday morning there would be a meeting followed by lunch, then a chance to explore the town on Saturday afternoon followed by a group dinner on the Saturday evening, probably with a speaker. On Sunday morning before coffee, there would be some internal business to complete, and the guests would leave after coffee. If any wished to stay for Sunday lunch, then they would have to book privately, and likewise if any wanted to extend their stay either before or after the conference, then it would be a private matter. Delegates would be allowed to bring their spouses, some of whom may go into town during the meetings or business discussions, but all delegates would pay their individual expenses.

Unlike a conference for a large business or company the firm would not pay. For Ivor, it sounded like a wonderful booking and the pleasure registered on his face.

'Yes, we can certainly accommodate your conference, and I shall send you a list of our charges, with a special conference rate if every room is booked. We will require a deposit for each room four weeks before the conference, that is standard procedure. I am sure you will realize we are trying to build a reputation for hosting small weekend conferences and I can assure you that your delegates will receive the very best of attention. To whom shall I send the information?'

The man gave an address and telephone number which Ivor wrote down, adding he would pencil in the dates with confirmation expected at least four weeks prior to the event – that confirmation would be receipt of the room deposits. The caller seemed quite happy with the arrangements, and then Ivor asked, 'Might I ask the name of your organization, sir?'

I did not hear the man's reply but he spoke for some time, then Ivor said, 'I understand perfectly, I am a retired police officer, and my hotel is noted for its security and confidentiality. And yes, of course you or any of your delegates may visit the hotel at any time in advance, in secret or openly to ensure the accuracy of my claims.' There was a small amount of further discussion after which Ivor replaced the phone. I noticed the large smile of success and pleasure on his face.

'That was the chairman of the Association of Permanent Parliamentary Personnel in London,' he beamed. 'They want to hold a weekend conference here. How about that?'

'Wonderful!' I tried to sound pleased for him. 'A block booking, your reputation must be spreading.'

'He said he had heard wonderful things about us from a Special Branch detective superintendent in the Met who'd come here for a week's holiday, and they think this hotel is just right for them. They want to get out of London and away from big cities, and don't wish to be bothered by the press or public. Discretion is what they seek in their hotels, and that's my speciality.'

'So who are they?'

'He said they are secretarial staff and managers who work in the Houses of Parliament on a permanent basis but they're not secretaries to Members of Parliament who disappear or arrive after elections. These people work permanently in the various departments and offices of the House of Commons.'

'Ah, I see. Civil servants, I suppose. So what does their association do?'

'It's a group of those admin staff who want to ensure that the work of the House continues in the event of civil unrest, strikes, sabotage or even war. They have lectures from experts in the police, armed services, security services and so forth, and their job is to maintain continuity of operations in spite of everything. They are taught how to deal with newspapers, strikers, unions and the general public.'

'So do the taxpayers fork out for this weekend shindig at your place?'

'No, he made that quite clear. The delegates pay their own expenses and those of their spouses who accompany them. It's not a trades union or official group, although in time they might develop into something very formal and official.'

'More like a group of friends perhaps?'

'Possibly, lots of these societies begin in a small way. At the moment, that one's fairly small but the chairman said it is partly social but nonetheless very professional due to the standing of the lecturers they attract. It's a band of dedicated staff, in other words. It sounds just the sort of people I can work with. It means, PC Rhea, that my reputation will be at the heart of the British establishment and who knows where that might lead? I shall be working among policy makers and those who run the country. This is such an important development and naturally, I shall produce a very favourable package for them.'

'Well, let's hope they honour the agreement.'

'I can't see a group like that backing out once the arrangements are made!'

And so, finding his register was in order, I left Ivor to bask in his personal success and continued my tour of duty. Over the months when I continued to work occasionally in Strensford, I would pop in to Beachview, sometimes to check the register and sometimes to pass on any relevant crime prevention advice that was current, and in those small ways I kept in touch with Ivor. He wasn't as miserable as his public image would suggest – in fact, he was very kind and thoughtful even if he did set his sights at the upper classes and wealthy and even if he did appear rather pompous and rule-bound at times. But he was efficient and ran a very smooth operation at his hotel. It was during those visits I learned that the Association of Permanent Parliamentary Personnel had confirmed their conference with every room booked and the necessary deposits paid.

Their chairman had even assured Ivor that if the hotel met with their expectations, they would return the following year. The current conference was on a weekend in April, during the Easter school holidays when Strensford's tourist season was getting under way. That weekend, I was once again plodding the streets, this time with no particular commitments. It was a Saturday, always a busy day in the town, and I was patrolling near the harbourside. As I stood on the edge of the wharf, enjoying the mild weather and splendid views, a young couple approached me. The man was about twenty-seven or eight, and the woman a couple of years his junior. Both were smartly but casually dressed.

'Hi.' The man smiled. 'I thought I'd introduce myself, I'm in the job. Ron Newton, this is my wife Sue, she's a secretary.'

'Ah, hello, I'm Nick Rhea.' We shook hands. 'So which force are you in?'

'The Met. Down in the smoke, as you rustics call it! Watching you just now and looking at the crowds, I was just thinking how peaceful it is up here in Yorkshire. In fact, it's something I've been thinking about for quite a while. This is the North Riding, isn't it? Very rural, not like the West Riding. So does your force accept transfers?'

'If there are vacancies, yes, but usually just in the constable rank. We don't want sergeants and above transferring in and taking up all the promotions! We reckon they're for the local lads! But, we do get quite a lot of constables, men and women, joining from the big cities – Birmingham, Manchester, the Met of course, all wanting a more peaceful way of earning a crust!'

'Well, I'm a constable in the West End, five years in the job so far and it's all hell and no notion down there. Work never stops, there's constant pressure, noise all the time, demonstrations, traffic, crowds, tourists and crime, lots of it.'

'I must admit it's a bit calmer up here!' I smiled. 'Some might say boring!'

'I know, and I've got to think of Sue, and perhaps a family one of these days. I want a good quality of life for us all. Since we got married a couple of years ago, Sue and I have spent a few holidays in this part of Yorkshire and now we both fancy working here. She's a civil servant, a trained secretary with shorthand and typing, so I'm sure she'd get a job with one of the councils or even in business. So, realistically, what are the chances of me getting a transfer?'

'Fairly good right now.' I knew the North Riding had a few vacancies for constables, having just won an increase in establishment from the Home Office. The force had been given authority to recruit twenty extra constables and it seemed this fellow might fill one of the vacancies. We chatted for a while about the type of work undertaken in a rural police force with me stressing we even dealt with diseases of animals and poachers. I told him about the small market towns, the seaside resorts, the remote villages and the vast open spaces of the dales and moors, not forgetting other differences such as our sergeants prosecuting in magistrates' courts, the fact that any constable arriving first at the scene of a sudden death became the coroner's officer for that particular case, our attendance at lots of race meetings within the county and the fact that the Metropolitan Police Act was not in force in the rural North Riding.

That was a catch-all statute widely used by London's Metropolitan Police Officers for dealing with a range of offenders – we had to know how to use various other statutes along with different powers of arrest. But for all the differences in our work patterns, however, the job was basically the same.

After my chat, he seemed very keen to join us and I gave him the address of Force Headquarters in Racecourse Lane at North-allerton, suggesting he wrote for a transfer application form which would provide him with all the information he required. He thanked me and hoped our paths would cross again, as they probably would if he decided to transfer to the North Riding.

'So where are you staying?' I asked.

'Beachview Private Hotel,' he said. 'Nice place, it's owned by an ex-Met sergeant, Ivor Bindwood. He runs it like clockwork. There's a party of us, we've taken the whole place. Nice and private.'

'Ah!' Then I recalled the Association of Permanent Parliamentary Personnel. 'You're with the Association of Permanent

Parliamentary Personnel?'

At the mention of that association, both he and his wife laughed aloud and I wondered what the joke was, then Ron said, 'There's no such thing, Nick. We're just a bunch of young Met coppers who like to get out of London once in a while, well away from work for the weekend. With our wives – or husbands in some cases – we hunt for nice small hotels which we can take over, then we can let our hair down and be ourselves, free from the constraints of the job. One of our detective supers recommended Beach-view, and he told us about Ivor who owns it.'

'Word of mouth is often the best recom-mendation!'

'Right, but Ivor doesn't know us, he didn't serve in our division but his reputation is very well known down in the smoke!'

'So what's all this about being the Asso-ciation of Permanent Parliamentary Person-nel?'

'You won't tell Ivor, will you?'

'Scout's Honour!' I laughed, and gave the three-fingered Scout salute.

'Well, if any hotel we book knew we were a bunch of off-duty coppers, we'd be on show all the time, unable to let our hair down, always having to behave and watch our behaviour and language, so because two of the wives of our members work in the House of Commons, as civil servants, we came up with this fictitious association. One of our women officers has a husband working there as well, so we decided to form ourselves into the association, it's a wonderful means of concealing our real jobs and enjoying ourselves at the same time. We pretend to have lectures and seminars but those meetings are really just to decide what we are going to do next time. The association travels all over – we went to Paris for a weekend, we've been to theatres in the West End, visited several popular towns in England, Wales and Scotland, and everywhere we go, we get special treatment.'

'I'm not surprised, having an association with a name like yours!'

'It worked with Ivor. You'd be amazed just how well he's treating us – we know all about the way he used to butter up to senior ranks in the job, but if he knew we were all just humble constables ... well, I think he might kick us out!'

'He might arrest you all for fraud and bring you into our station!'

'But we are a genuine association, thanks to some of our wives. You know, that would be one thing I'd miss if I transferred to Yorkshire. The fellowship we have in the association.'

'You could always set up a Yorkshire Branch of the Association of Permanent Parliamentary Personnel,' I suggested. 'Not that we have many parliamentary personnel working up here!'

'You'd enjoy meeting us all, and I'd invite you back to the hotel tonight but all the table places are taken. I'm sure there will be other times.'

'Well, I don't live in Strensford, I'm really the village constable at Aidensfield a few miles from here and so it wouldn't be easy, staying in town and then having to drive home. But thanks and the best of luck with your transfer application.'

And so it was that I realized Ivor Bindwood, the man who reckoned he could smell a fraudster a mile off, was acting as host to a lot of constables and treating them like VIPs. I hoped he never found out.

The most important aspects of being a confidence trickster were personal appearance and a smart line in believable patter. Some of these scoundrels could produce an amazing line of patter during a conversation which would convince the listener that the villain was a massively successful business-man, a worldwide entrepreneur, member of the aristocracy, friend of the royal family, famous actor or indeed anything else.

To support the claims, the trickster's clothing had to reflect his or her false image. I recall a notorious confidence trickster who preyed on gullible but wealthy women in smart hotels. His tale was that he came from an aristocratic background, and the false names he used would reflect this. In a splendid accent, he would talk of the family estates here and overseas and he supported his claim by having a monogrammed gold cigarette case and matching cufflinks. His blazer had a coat of arms on the pocket and his tie sported a copy of it; there was often a gold tie-pin in his ties too, and his clothing always had an air of absolute quality. He wore only the best and stayed at the best hotels. That the fellow was stylish and plausible was never in doubt and yet he was a notorious confidence trick-ster who wheedled his way into the affections of gullible women, and then persuaded them to part with lots of money as a temporary loan to him, which he would promise to repay with a high rate of interest when his vast inheritance from Lord Somebody-Or-

Other was finalized. Once he had the money safe in his possession, he vanished.

In another case, I remember a confidence trickster being arrested and appearing at our local court on several charges of false pretences; he was convicted and sentenced to a short term of imprisonment. A local constable had the task of escorting the fellow to prison, and in those days this was sometimes done by train, the prisoner being handcuffed to the police officer during the journey. And on the hour-long journey by train, that prisoner persuaded the policeman to give him five pounds 'for his granny who, after Grandad's death, was desperately short of money and was now threatened with eviction from her home if she didn't pay her back-rent.'

Whilst some of us might grudgingly admire confidence tricksters for their doubtful skills and the fact they seldom use violence, there are those who place the blame for the offences upon their silly, rich victims, some believing they deserve everything that befalls them if they fall for such a confidence trick. Most of us know that if something sounds too good to be true, it probably is!

Nonetheless, we tend to trust people who are smartly dressed while being rather wary of those who are scruffy. There is no doubt many of us respond positively to a person's clothing – if someone wears a police uniform, we presume he or she is a police officer; the same applies if a person wears a military uniform, nurse's outfit or some other very recognizable clothing. Very rarely do we question their authenticity. This has been proved time and time again by fraudsters entering hospitals and simply walking about while wearing a white coat, even to the extent of attending operations. I remember one character who stole a service bus, donned the driver's cap which was in the cab and then drove it along a well-known route to collect passengers. After driving to the edge of town, the last passenger disembarked whereupon the driver then abandoned the bus – and left with a few pounds personal profit!

I must admit I never gave this a thought as I was patrolling the promenade, a public walkway at the foot of the cliffs in Strensford. It was a wide stone path which separated the beach from the base of the cliffs, and the section closest to the cliffs bore dozens of brightly painted beach huts.

There were regular flights of steps down to the sands every two hundred yards or so, usually with deckchair sellers or ice cream vendors nearby. On this occasion, I spotted a noticeboard which had been stuck in the sands on a long pole. I had never seen it before, but that might be due to the fact that a duty patrol on this area was not very common. Not many police officers patrolled this close to the beach, but I felt it necessary once in a while; after all, people lost their purses and wallets and children got lost, so there was frequently work for the police.

The large noticeboard was painted dark green with clear white lettering and was about a hundred yards from the foot of a flight of steps, midway between the walkway and the edge of the sea. The tide was out so there ample space around it. The lettering said, 'Open Air Church Service here at 11 a.m. All welcome. Bring your family, friends, dogs and ice creams. It will last for only twenty minutes, there will be some singing and prayers, and a warm welcome is guaranteed.'

I had never previously encountered a beach service although I knew that some people actually got married on the beach in sunny countries overseas and I was aware that, on very special occasions, a service of some kind might be held on the shore. There was, for example, an annual Blessing of the Boats ceremony in Strensford, with the bandstand on the harbourside also being a venue for lots of religious events. In the latter cases, a brass band was usually present to liven things up with well-known hymns – as the name of the location suggested. I glanced at my watch. It was ten minutes to eleven and I had no commitments, so I decided to stay to find out more about the event, at the same time moving a little closer to obtain a better view.

Below the noticeboard I could see a small wooden box with a slit in the lid and above it was another sign, a smaller one saying, 'For Church Funds'. Very quickly, I became aware of a tall dark-haired man who was wearing a black suit. He was walking among the holidaymakers as they sat or played on the beach, speaking to them and then pointing to the noticeboard. He spent several minutes moving among them, chatting with both good humour and some persuasion because several rose to their feet, clad in bathing costumes, and drifted towards the noticeboard. As they began to assemble before it, others followed and then, just before eleven o'clock, the man dragged an empty bottle crate across the beach and stood upon it. I could now see he was wearing a dog collar.

As the people began to gather before him, I saw he was carrying a bell in one hand, holding it by the clapper to prevent it ringing, but then he released his grip and started to wave the bell in huge sweeps of his arm. Its strong sound was louder than any of the other beach noises and he began to shout, 'Come and join us, come and join us, everyone welcome'. Somewhat reluctantly, more holidaymakers, including children and dogs, wandered across to see what the fuss was about and then he called, 'Now we shall sing our first hymn. Everyone join in. It is "All Creatures Great and Small".' And with that, he placed the bell on the ground, flipped a sheet of paper from the back of his noticeboard over to the front and I could see it bore the words of the hymn.

His next trick was to produce a harmonica from his pocket and I heard the distinctive tune of 'All Creatures Great and Small' wafting towards me over the sound of the waves.

At this stage, the people began to sing, a strange mixture of harmonica, voices on the wind and the crashing of waves in the background.

I decided it was time to leave. I could see that his performance had cleared a large patch of the beach but as the sands were more than two miles long with hundreds if not thousands of people enjoying the seaside, there were many more sites for him to exploit. It would take him almost all day to persuade everyone to join him for a few minutes, and, of course, the incoming tide would determine just how far he could operate and how long he could stay. I did not recognize the clergyman but that was not surprising, me being almost a stranger to the town.

Having left this rather pleasing aspect of beach life, I wandered back into streets to resume a more normal type of patrol. My patch that day included the harbourside and town centre where I would remain until 1 p.m., after which I would have my 45-minute refreshment break before continuing until 5 p.m. It would be a pleasant day's work among happy holidaymakers.

I was not scheduled to pay a return visit to the beach – for one thing the tide would have turned and would now be clearing the holidaymakers as it rose towards the cliffs – but part of my patrol included the harbourside and bandstand. And there, as large as life on his box in the middle of the bandstand, was the beach preacher, playing his mouth organ with one hand and conducting with the other while the people stood around and sang 'How Great Thou Art'. I stood at a distance and watched, marvelling how the communal singing drew others towards the centre of events.

I realized that, before the end of this little service, there would be a crowd of at least a hundred, probably more.

On this occasion, however, I had arrived at the end of his service and I saw him hold up the money box and called, 'Show your faith in the Lord by helping to spread his word.' And he rattled the box before replacing it on the ground. Most of the crowd popped money into the box before leaving, although some merely drifted away. As I stood and observed from a distance, I calculated he must have held at least six services that day, even seven or eight depending upon when he started. I made my guess that he'd undertake one per hour from 10 a.m. or even 9 a.m. depending upon how far he had travelled.

Although each service was only twenty minutes or so in duration, he had to transfer himself and his belongings from site to site, assemble his congregation and then allow time for them to disperse afterwards or linger awhile to chat to him. I estimated there would be between fifty and a hundred at each service – with perhaps more on the bandstand but fewer at each beach venue – but if, say, seventy on average gave only a modest donation of sixpence, that would be £1 15s 0d. per service. That rough calculation meant that eight services could net him something like £14 0s. 0d. per day, rather more than a whole week's wage for me, although in his case he would have incurred expenses for his visit. It still left a nice income for his church.

As I was due to conclude my shift at 5 p.m., I began to wend my way back through the streets but en route I passed St Hilda's Roman Catholic Church.

The parish priest, whom I did not know, was outside painting the iron railings which bordered the tiny patch of garden. As I strode past, I said, 'Good-afternoon, Father, nice job you've got there!'

'Hello, Constable.' He stood up and flexed his back. 'It's back-breaking work, but it has to be done. You're not one of our local constables?'

He made the statement almost as a question and so I stopped for a chat.

'No, I'm from Aidensfield; just here for

the day to fill a gap.'

'Ah, Aidensfield, very close to Maddles-kirk Abbey!'

'Yes, I'm a Catholic. PC Rhea,' I told him. 'But surely you could have persuaded a parishioner to paint these for you?'

'I've tried. They promise all the help in the world but never get round to doing it! We can't afford a professional painter, funds are always tight, so I decided to do it myself. Actually, I'm quite enjoying it; it makes a change from writing sermons and trying to explain the gospel. It might even produce a theme for one of my homilies.'

'You ought to do what that clergyman was doing on the beach today,' I smiled.

'And what might that be?'

'Holding beach services, one every hour or so I think, getting the holidaymakers to sing hymns and say a few prayers, then collecting donations ... it seemed to work.'

'What did he look like?' There was concern in his face now. 'Did you see him?'

'Yes.' And so I described the man, saying I had no idea to which church he belonged, but he appeared to have the knack of persuading the public to join him. I added, 'He was near the far end of the beach this morning, and then this afternoon he was on the bandstand, I think he had been on other parts of the beach too.'

'The man's a charlatan!' he snapped.

'A charlatan?'

'A confidence trickster, no less! He's no clergyman, Constable; he's no more a priest, vicar or minister than a dog is! He puts on a dog collar and a dark suit, goes onto the beach, persuades the people to join him in hymns and prayers, and then takes a collection. For himself. Not for any church. He's been doing it for years on northern beaches but because he moves around a lot, we never know where he is.'

'Have the police been informed?'

'On and off, yes, but this has been going on for years, PC Rhea. All churches in the coastal resorts, Catholic and Protestant, have been warned about him but we haven't the time to hang about the beaches and harbours on the off-chance he'll turn up. And neither have you. On top of that, no one knows who he is or where he comes from.'

'Neither do I and I must admit I had no idea he was a fraud. He certainly looked the part and he did get the people to join in.'

'Well, I suppose there is some good in that, PC Rhea. After all, he's not doing any harm to anyone but he's a trickster, take my word for it.'

'We could only proceed against him if we received a formal complaint from one of the people who might consider themselves tricked into giving him money on some pretext, but I suppose in some ways he's no different from any other street or beach entertainer. Like a Punch-and-Judy man or juggler or singer. If people give money voluntarily in return for services rendered, it might cause problems in court on the grounds the alleged victims were not tricked into parting with it. They gave it voluntarily and who is to say he's not giving it to some church?'

'I appreciate all that, which is probably why he has never been prosecuted. He might not be actually committing any crime and he is getting the people to pray and think of God, so I suppose he might be doing some good. But he is not a priest, PC Rhea. All the coastal churches have carried out checks and so far as anyone knows, he doesn't belong to any organized religion. He's never turned up in any of our churches, that's for sure.'

'I'll have a quick walk back to the bandstand to see if he's still around, and if he is, I'll have words with him,' I promised.

But there was no sign of the fake clergyman. When I returned to the station to book off duty, I told Sergeant Mason of this development, but he merely shrugged his shoulders.

'We can't take action unless we receive a formal complaint,' he said. 'Are you going to lodge a formal complaint, PC Rhea?'

'No, I didn't give him any money,' was my reply, although I had to admit I thought he was genuine.

'But would you have complained if you had donated, say, threepence or sixpence to his church before realizing he was a con man?'

'No, not for such a small amount.'

'Well, there's your answer. People will have given a few pence because he entertained them. There's nothing illegal in that.'

'But he was a fraud, sergeant.'

'Do they know that, and if they did, are they likely to complain?'

'Probably not.'

'Well, he's got a few holidaymakers to think about church and religion. He must have done some good. God works in mysterious ways,' said the smiling sergeant.

CHAPTER 6

Continuing the topic of entertainers, I was always fascinated, in my childhood years, by conjurors and card magicians who, by sheer sleight of hand, could work apparent miracles before my very eyes. I never doubted that the speed of the hand could deceive the eye, and I now know that saying is absolutely true. Even if the magic of television and technology can produce miracles and illusions, the speed of the hand can still deceive the eye. Fired with juvenile enthusiasm as I matured into my late teens, I thought I would like to perform card tricks and so I bought books such as The Royal Road to Card Magic and Advanced Card Technique. These were followed by other books and catalogues about specialized branches of the craft such as stage illusions, tricks with coins, cigarettes and ropes, vanishing bowls of water, rabbits and doves, and a host of others.

Armed with all this guidance, along with books advising beginners how to stage a small show before an audience, I settled down to teach myself some card flourishes and tricks. Soon, I had mastered a few but meanwhile had learned how to produce a string of razor blades from my mouth, produce silks from an empty box and pluck cards from thin air; I could perform the famous chinese rings trick and multiply billiard balls in an empty hand. Although I had no wish to perform in public, it didn't take long for my hobby to become known to a few who then asked if I would entertain at local concerts or parties and so, somewhat reluctantly, I found myself on stage doing all the things I'd seen others do when I was a child.

If any advantages came from this, it was that I had to overcome my natural shyness and learn to communicate with an audience – a useful skill in later life. I continued to practice those skills as a young constable at Aidensfield, performing at police Christmas celebrations and birthday parties for my own children, in the meantime buying more equipment which would enable me to entertain children – the most enthusiastic but most critical of all audiences! If anyone can spot how a trick is performed, it will be a sharp-eyed child who will announce it to the entire audience.

As time progressed, however, the demands of work and particularly the difficulties of getting time off due to shift work and the fact I was getting older with other commitments, meant my conjuring skills had to be restricted mainly to the home. Police duties and outside commitments do not readily mix, especially when responsible for a rural beat for twenty-four hours per day. Even when undertaking shift work in towns, my police job always took precedence and, of course, I never knew what unexpected dramas and events were awaiting immediate attention. Even if some fairly routine incident such as a traffic accident or sudden death occurred after I had finished work for the day at Aidensfield, I would have to deal with it. That was the situation even if it meant cancelling a twenty-minute conjuring display at the local Women's Institute's Christmas party.

It was against this fading background that I found myself patrolling Strensford during the peak of the holiday season. The town had a Spa Theatre which hosted a range of evening events from variety shows to plays via classical music and brass band concerts, along with afternoon tea dances and easy-listening musical treats.

These were always popular with visitors and residents alike, but, in addition there were other concert venues. One of the larger hotels hosted a range of regular events from dinner dances to musical evenings for smaller audiences whilst one of the larger church halls was always busy with craft fairs, amateur shows and pantomimes. There were three cinemas too, along with working men's clubs and cafes which boasted a pianist on Saturday evenings and Sunday lunchtimes. Some of the variety shows attracted well-known artistes, occasionally for just one special evening but sometimes for an entire week or even a season. We might have the services of say, a well-known or even famous musician, singer or group of singers, dance band, comedian, star of stage or screen, juggler, dancer, trapeze artiste or, of course, a magician specializing in perhaps grand illusions such as making a person levitate or even thrusting swords through a cabinet containing a pretty girl in a scanty costume.

While a production was either in rehearsal or performing, it was not uncommon for policemen to be invited behind the scenes for a while, usually because the uniform acted as a deterrent to the more enthusiastic and determined fans who might otherwise attempt to gatecrash the proceedings. Generally, of course, the stage door itself was a safeguard but sometimes ardent fans in the audience or even during rehearsals could dodge the attendants and climb onto the stage, even during a performance. If there was no performance, some tried to gain access to the dressing-rooms during rehearsals. The trouble was that some fans didn't know the difference between a real copper and an actor in uniform.

By and large, however, this unofficial system appeared to be satisfactory even if attention to the security of the theatre was really not a formal part of our duties. Undertaking this kind of liaison was really a matter for private security services or the theatre management, but in truth it was one of those grey areas where we tried to help because even the merest sight of a police officer in uniform could help to preserve the peace and avoid future problems. Nipping something in the proverbial bud could often prevent a more dangerous or dramatic incident.

Apart from that, being backstage during a performance on a cold and wet night was a wonderful way of sheltering from the worst of the coastal weather which could even arrive during the summer on the east coast! Such shelter was especially welcome as cups of tea and coffee were always in plentiful supply Another bonus was that the artistes were always pleasant even if they were doing their best to learn lines or rehearse routines under considerable pressure. And I should add that I never encountered tantrums or ego trips.

One summer while seconded to Strensford during the summer season, the Excelsior Hotel had decided to provide rather select entertainment during afternoon tea. It would serve tea and cakes in the Heather Room from 3 p.m. until 4.30 p.m., but in addition there would be carefully selected short entertainments whose purpose would be to make teatime more enjoyable. Those entertainments would change regularly between Easter and the end of September, but they might include, for example, a pianist, a violinist, a harpist, a string quartet, various singers and comedians, a magician, a dancer, a ventriloquist and even a mime artist.

Each turn would have the floor to themselves with a small audience of perhaps sixty or seventy at the most, and each performance would last for no longer than half an hour.

Advance publicity informed potential audience members which of the acts was performing at a particular time so they could purchase the necessary tickets and the idea received a warm preview in the *Strensford Gazette*. When I discovered that Jack Diamond, the well-known Yorkshire card magic expert, was one of the invited entertainers, I was determined to go along to watch him. His name was widely known in the clubs and concert halls of the north, for he had been a popular entertainer for several years, never quite hitting the top spot in a variety show, but always there as a reliable supporter or solo act. Fortunately, I was scheduled for a week of early turn duties in the town during August – that meant starting my patrols at 6 a.m. and finishing at 2 p.m., thus giving me an opportunity to take tea at the Excelsior while watching the famous cardman in action – and at fairly close quarters. Naturally, I wanted to meet him to chat about our mutual interest but didn't feel I should intrude upon his privacy, nor indeed his generosity. Nonetheless, I felt I'd never get another chance to meet him, so what should I do? I didn't want to waylay him, nor did I want to appear like a fawning fan.

Fate provided the solution. On the Monday of that week in Strensford, I was called to the Excelsior because someone had broken into one of the third-floor staff bedrooms and stolen a money box containing somewhere around £25-£30 in cash. The single bedroom, like all bedrooms on that floor, was occupied by a staff member.

On this occasion one of the waitresses, Marie Fowler, occupied the room which had been attacked and the stolen money represented several weeks' tips which she had saved over the months so that she could buy nice clothes or have a special holiday.

When I arrived, Marie was in the manager's office with her boss, Alan Briggs, and coffee had been prepared in anticipation of my arrival. Marie was a young woman of about twenty-two with a pleasant face, neat hair and a slender figure. Clearly, she was upset by the raid upon her property and also the invasion of her privacy, but as I gently questioned her, she was able to provide a clear account.

It appeared the thief had climbed the fire-escape outside her room and had smashed the window glass, released the catch and climbed in during Sunday night while Marie was absent. She had been working between 6 p.m. and 11.30 p.m. and after getting washed and changed, had gone out to a nightclub with a friend, staying the night at the friend's flat. She discovered the break-in when she returned at 9 a.m. for work that Monday morning and so it was likely the crime had occurred after Marie had left for the club on Sunday night but before her return on Monday. The fact it was the only break-in at the hotel that night suggested the culprit knew that Marie was away but also that she kept quite a large amount of cash in her room. The cash, although originally in the coins she had received as tips, had been changed into notes by Marie because they took up less space in her money box, so the thief would now have a wallet or purse full of pound notes and ten-shilling notes. She said there were no fivers among them.

In my view, the indications were that the thief was familiar with the hotel routine, and fairly closely acquainted with Marie. It would mean questioning every member of staff to determine their whereabouts at the material time, and for that I would need assistance from Alan Briggs. I hoped to receive his confidential opinion about anyone who might be responsible.

He should know his workers' weaknesses, relationships or capacity for revenge if there had been an internal dispute. I would also have to find out whether any of them were in desperate financial straits, or had any other reason for targetting Marie's savings. Motives like jealousy or revenge could not be ignored. First, though, having briefly examined the room from the doorway without entering or interfering with any fingerprints or other evidence that might be present, I decided to call in the Scene of Crime officers. I felt they should examine the room, especially the window, fire escape and wardrobe from which the money had been taken. On those places in particular, there may be fingerprints and other evidence. I could use the hotel's telephone to call SOCO and if fingerprints were found, then we might have to take the prints of all the staff if only for elimination purposes.

I realized that some staff, such as cleaners, chambermaids and the receptionist would have master keys to all rooms whilst others may also have access to such a key, so why go to the trouble of breaking in? Was that a decoy move, or was the culprit a staff member who did not have access to a room key? I could see there were lots of inquiries to be made and so, having questioned Marie as far as possible, I asked her to await the Scenes of Crime officers before doing anything else in her room.

The manager said she could usefully occupy herself by helping to clear the dining-room after breakfast and continue by setting it up for lunch. I told her I'd be on the premises for some time and would keep her informed about the result of my inquiries.

I started by requesting a list of all staff members, particularly those who were on the premises, either at work or at leisure, on Sunday night or Monday morning, and I felt sure the mode of entry suggested a man. Using that logic as my starting point, I would begin with all male staff members who would not have access to a room key and the manager provided the necessary names. Then I would question female members. And I also asked for a list of everyone, staff or guests, using the rooms adjoining Marie's – they might have seen or heard someone on the fire escape at an odd hour of the night, or heard the noise of breaking glass. And had the thief made his exit through the room door instead of de-scending the fire escape? As the bedrooms were fitted with Yale locks, the bedroom doors could be opened from the inside with-out keys, to re-lock themselves on closure. That seemed very likely – by emerging from a bedroom, the thief would not draw attention to himself by walking normally along a hotel corridor.

Then there were staff members who did not reside in the hotel, but who came in on a daily basis, some arriving very early to prepare breakfast, and others working late into the night. It looked like being a long inquiry and I hoped my bosses would allow me the necessary time to make a good job of it.

Alan Briggs, a most helpful manager, allocated me a small room and allowed me to call in staff members at my own discretion; he said he had no wish to sit in the interviews, believing they would speak more freely to me if he was not present. I felt he was right. Doing my best not to disrupt the hotel's busy routine, I managed to isolate and interview, one by one, those male members of staff currently on the premises, and then the females. There were far more females than males.

In the meantime, Scene of Crime arrived to begin their expert examination of the room, window and fire escape and I briefed them. Things were moving along quite nicely, I felt, and although I was getting nowhere near to identifying the thief I felt sure I was eliminating all the innocent staff one by one. Everyone I spoke to could explain their movements, and most had been with friends who could verify their statements. Furthermore, I found no one with a grudge against Marie, and no one who would know of her secret hoard. It was a secret hoard; she assured me no one else knew about it.

As I continued my inquiries, the Scene of Crime officer's examined the room in great detail; obviously, the room would contain Marie's own prints, and probably those of others who had used it, either as visitors or residents and a process of elimination would necessarily follow. Later, I was to learn that the windowpane, the catch, the wardrobe and other places likely to be touched by the raider did not produce any results. If the raider had been careless, a matching set of prints would have been found on those areas, but there was nothing. The raider appeared to have been very careful.

Having spoken to all the staff currently on the premises, either at work or resting, I turned my attention to the occupants of rooms near Marie's. There were three in which I was interested – one at either side, both occupied by staff and another directly beneath Marie's on the second floor. The ground-floor room at the foot of the fire escape was a storeroom with no window or door opening onto the passage outside so there was no need to concern myself with that one.

When I checked the names on my list, I saw I had already spoken to the staff members who used the adjoining rooms, so that left only the one directly below Marie's. I went to speak to Alan Briggs once again, asking who occupied it.

'It's a Mr Gordon Dewhirst,' he told me. 'Actually, he's our entertainer for this week, the card man. You might have seen him billed as Jack Diamond. He's a very nice man with no hint of an ego. It's room 5 on the second floor. He often rehearses in his room.'

'Can you let him know I'd like to talk to him? I would hate to disturb him if he's in the middle of something difficult.'

'Sure, I'll send someone up.' There were no telephones in the guests' rooms so he called a maid.

'Sally, go to Mr Dewhirst's room, will you, and tell him PC Rhea would like a chat, about Marie's missing money.'

'Yes, Mr Briggs,' she said, galloping away upon her errand. Minutes later she returned, smiled and said I could go up immediately. I climbed the stairs, found the room and tapped on the door.

'Come!' shouted a loud clear voice. 'The door's unlocked.'

I went in to see Mr Dewhirst producing a fistful of cards apparently out of thin air, one of the tricks I could do, and one which required considerable dexterity. As he was in the middle of that rehearsal, I waited until he had finished; that was when he threw the last cards onto his bed and smiled.

'All right, was it, Constable? You chaps are supposed to be sharp-eyed and very observant, so do you think our teatime people will like that one?'

He was a fairly tall man with rather square features and jet-black hair smartly cut and well cared for. He was powerfully built too, and I guessed he would be in his late forties. He looked more like a sergeant-major than a professional magician although his hands had long, slender fingers.

'A nice starter, I always think,' I smiled. 'It gets the audience puzzling right from the start, grabs their attention.'

'You know about these things?' He sounded surprised.

'It's my hobby,' I told him. 'I do the occasional small show; and usually start with

214

that trick, pulling cards apparently out of thin air.'

'Show me,' he said, and picked up another pack of cards which he tossed over to me. I abstracted them, fanned them and was pleased to find they had been treated with zinc stearate; this was a powder which made their surfaces slippery, rather like dry soap flakes were spread on dance floors to produce a similar smoothing effect for the dancers' feet. With the cards treated like this, they could be fanned smoothly or used to create wonderful displays and flourishes.

These cards were well used too, which made them soft and pliable, another bonus.

Although I was here on a crime inquiry, I felt this might establish a rapport between us and so I pulled up my tunic and shirt sleeves, took the cards in my right hand, held it high and made the entire pack vanish. Then I pulled some out of thin air, showed my hand to be empty apart from those cards, and dropped them on the floor, only to produce another handful. I did this several times and then stopped by throwing the last few onto the floor. He applauded.

'Look,' he said, 'that was good, and at close quarters too. I have a proposition for you, but first, you'd better tell me your business! I assume you're not here to discuss card magic with me!'

I explained about the raid on Marie Fowler's room, pointing out that the fire escape passed very close to his window, and asked whether he had heard anything unusual during the late night or early hours. He listened carefully but shook his head.

'Sorry,' he apologized. 'I had a drink at the bar, a small whisky before coming to bed, and that would be about half-past eleven. The barman said he was open until midnight, but I didn't want to stay up that late. I came in here and was asleep the minute my head touched the pillow. Nothing disturbed me during the night, Constable, nothing at all. Sorry.'

'Fine,' I said. 'I'm just trying to establish the precise time of the break-in, but thanks, I'll keep asking...'

'Right, now I've a proposition for you but first tell me about the other card routines you can do. Or other tricks if you do them. And what's your name?'

I told him, then outlined the card routines with which I felt confident and showed him my abilities with more packs of his cards, adding I could perform the chinese ring trick and several others which did not use playing cards.

'Right, when are you off duty?'

'I finish at two, normally I go straight home but I've made plans to come and see you,' I said, adding that I lived some distance away from Strensford.

'Really, I am flattered! Look, I'll be backstage half an hour before the show starts, preparing, rehearsing, checking my equipment, you know the routine. Why don't you come along directly after your shift, and join me? You can be there as my assistant. But there's a catch.'

'Catch?'

'A friend of mine died last week, it's his funeral on Thursday afternoon but I can't attend because I'm committed here. So how about you doing the Thursday show for me? You could dress up in my gear – I dress like the Jack of Diamonds you see on a pack of cards, colourful cloak, long blond wig, red hat ... you're about my size. And all you need do is a half-hour show of your own choice. It would mean I could attend the funeral and you'd be Jack Diamond for half an hour. Or I have a Jack of Spades costume if you'd prefer that...'

'Me?' I was astonished. 'But I'm not up to your standard ... and wouldn't it be deceitful, me pretending to be you!'

'Not if we announced it in advance ... I'd square things between me and the hotel, I'd say my deputy was Jack of Spades, and you'd get my fee too. So how about it? Half an hour, that's all it would take. And a bit of rehearsal. And it would mean I could say a proper farewell to an old pal.'

'Well, I'm not sure...' beneath my uniform my heart was beating loud and fast. I knew I could keep a small audience entertained – I'd done it many times – but could I honestly deputize for a man of his renown, skill and experience? That was a different matter all together, although, of course, each audience would be a new one. My audience would not have seen him in action and so comparisons might not be something to worry about. Or did the same people take afternoon tea every day of the week? Would the regulars attend every show?

'I won't press you for an answer now. Go away and think about it,' he suggested. 'Then come back this afternoon and act as my assistant, we can talk it over then. You can use my props if you want, or you could bring your own. But it would enable me to see a dear friend off to his heavenly paradise.'

'I'll think about it,' I promised. 'See you

218

this afternoon.'

I had not forgotten I was investigating a nasty crime and returned to the manager to report my progress, or lack of it. But Jack Diamond had given me an idea. I made my way to Alan Briggs's office.

'Any joy?' he asked.

'Not a thing, Mr Dewhirst heard nothing. But what about the barman?'

'What about him?' frowned Briggs.

'I've not spoken to him yet and he was working late, I believe.'

'Yes, he doesn't live-in, which is why you've not interviewed him, and he won't come on duty until five this afternoon. You'll know that bars in hotels are not tied to licensing hours so far as hotel residents are concerned, so it's usually midnight when he closes, sometimes later. He works the late shift, another chap does lunchtimes.'

'So there's more than one barman?'

'Yes, we use several, sometimes working solo and sometimes two or three together if we've a big event on, like a wedding. Some of them are merely temporary though. Sundays are usually very quiet. This chap works Sundays, name of Dave Cotterell. He's new to us, he came a week or two ago when the previous one left.'

'So where can I find him?'

'I'll have his address in my records.'

'So what's his routine? About locking up, I mean. I'm wondering if he might have seen or heard something out of the ordinary if he was working late.'

'You could always ask him,' he said. 'He cashes up and puts the money in the safe. In here, in my office. I've not checked last night's takings yet,' he said. 'It's been one of those mornings, non-stop! We check the takings around now in fact, then take it to the bank, less a twenty pound float the incoming barman will need for lunchtime...'

He found a key in one of his desk drawers and opened a cupboard in the wall to reveal a large, dark green safe with a brass combination lock.

Expertly turning the lock backwards and forwards, I heard the clicks and then the mighty door swung open.

'Oh my God!' he said. 'It's gone!'

'What has?'

'The bar cash box! The takings – Saturday and Sunday...'

'And who knew the combination apart from you?'

'He did. And my deputy. No one else.'

'Right,' I said. 'We need to find him pretty

quickly. Can you give me his address and a description of him, and any details of a vehicle he might be using? Even if he's not guilty, he needs to be eliminated from inquiries, and so does your deputy. I'll ring our office and get him circulated straight away. And I'll have to recall our Scene of Crime team, so don't touch anything.'

'This is dreadful...'

'So how much do you reckon there would be in here?'

'Well, we bank Friday's takings on Saturday morning, so there's two night's takings on a Monday morning ... four hundred pounds give or take a few quid, all in cash.'

'And unidentifiable!' I said. 'I am just wondering if he would bother to steal Marie's savings if he had access to all that cash?'

'Who knows? Maybe he was desperate for money, maybe he had some arrangement with the burglar and let him in, then gave him details of the safe's combination number ... I just don't know!'

'I need to talk to your deputy too, but first I must have another chat with Marie,' I told him. 'Just to see whether she has any reason to think the barman might be responsible.'

'God, this is dreadful. Right. I'll call her.'

When I questioned Marie, I could see her

eyes lighting up with renewed suspicion.

'He would often ask me for change,' she said. 'Sometimes when he was working, he would be short of small change and one night I said I had some in my room, tips I'd saved. I liked to have notes in my box, they don't take up as much room as coins, and they're not so heavy.'

'Did this happen a lot?' I asked.

'Quite often,' she admitted. And sometimes, I would take my change down to him, to swop for ten shilling notes or pound notes, so it worked both ways.'

'So here we have a barman who knew about your cache of money. Did he know you would be out of your room all last night?'

She nodded. 'I'd forgotten when you asked me before, but yes, I told him I was going to a club with a friend, straight from work, and I'd be out all night, staying with Jenny. He'd once recommended the Green Popinjay as a decent place to go, it's open till three in the morning, and so I told him I was going there with Jenny and I'd not be back till morning ... I thought he was a really nice man.'

'We need to talk to David Cotterell very urgently, and we need to check his fingerprints too. And to see if he has a record!'

Alan Briggs was still in a state of near disbelief.

'Look, Alan, I'll have to return to our police office with this news, I need to circulate details of Cotterell, and because of this development, CID might be called in to take over.'

'And I'll have to report this to my bosses, the owners. They won't be pleased! They keep on at us about security, especially with cash ... heads might roll! God, I could be for the high jump!'

'Right, well, I'll do what I must at the station, and will keep in touch. And keep out of that safe until SOCO arrive.'

Furnished with a good description of Cotterell and his private car along with his last known address, I hurried back to Strensford Police Station and informed Sergeant Mason of those developments.

'Right.' He smiled. 'Good work, Nick. Look, we should call CID but there's no reason why you shouldn't have the benefit of making this arrest, if the fellow's still at that address. Take the car and go up there now, and while you're away I'll circulate a description of Cotterell and his car, and I'll check CRO to see if he has form. And we'd better run checks on Alan Briggs and the rest of his staff.'

When I arrived at his address, I discovered it was a flat; the middle-aged lady owner lived in the ground-floor rooms and when I explained my inquiry she said, 'So that's it! He's gone, PC Rhea, he went out to work last night as usual, but this morning there was no sign of him, and when I checked because I didn't hear him moving around, I found his room was empty. Gone. Everything, his wardrobe and drawers are empty. And he owes me two weeks' rent.'

'Have you any idea where he's gone?'

'Not a clue. He never talked about himself, although there was a man looking for him last Friday, a nasty looking individual. When I told Mr Cotterell, he looked shocked but said nothing. Anyway, he's gone, and don't ask me where!'

'We've put an all stations message out for him and his car,' I said, explaining about the money missing from the hotel and Marie Fowler's room. 'If we find him, I'll let you know.'

'I'll wring his neck, so help me,' she said. 'I can't afford to carry passengers like him!'

With preliminary CRO checks showing Alan Briggs, his deputy and other staff members had no criminal records, I ret-urned to the hotel, interviewed the deputy manager to eliminate him from this inquiry and then found that a detective sergeant and a detective constable had arrived to take over the investigation. I had a quick word with Alan Briggs and Marie Fowler to explain what was happening and promised I would keep them informed of any further developments. By the time all that activity had ceased, it was time to book off duty - and pay my visit to Jack Diamond at the Excelsior after first ringing Mary to say I might be home later than expected.

Although I was still wearing my uniform shirt and trousers, albeit with a civilian jacket, he seemed unconcerned by my appearance. Tomorrow, I would bring some civilian clothes to change into.

I found Gordon very welcoming and he suggested I stand backstage to watch his final rehearsals, then join the audience to see him in action. I did so, and must admit I knew how he performed all his tricks, even if his expertise was far greater than mine. He was a consummate professional, wooing his audience and persuading them not to chatter while he was in action. He achieved that by walking among the tables, getting people to choose cards or check that he had nothing up his sleeve; in other words getting his audience involved. And they loved it. I learned a lot merely by watching him.

'Well, Nick, what do you think about my suggestion?'

'I can do all the tricks,' I said. 'But not up to your standard.'

'Well, you've got three days in which to rehearse. Well, not three full days, but enough time to make a good job of it. You can come and watch me and, if you want, then I'll put you through the entire routine with me as your audience. I can be critical, but helpful with it. After seeing you in action earlier, without any warning or rehearsal, I've got faith in you. I wouldn't have asked otherwise. It's only a half-hour show and if you like doing card magic, I'd say you'd find the whole thing highly enjoyable.'

And so it was that I stood in for Jack Diamond at the Excelsior that Thursday afternoon. Having watched him in action on Monday, Tuesday and Wednesday, I had gained sufficient knowledge of his techniques and banter to emulate him, and I felt sure that with all that rehearsal and guidance from him, I could master my craft.

In heavy disguise as Jack Spade complete

with wig and all-enveloping costume, I took a deep breath and began my act before an audience of around sixty people, mainly elderly, who were eating cakes and drinking tea. Although I recognized one or two people in the audience, they did not appear to recognize me. By copying his rapport with the audience at their tea-tables, I prevented them from chattering and the half-hour went surprisingly quickly. Next day, having heard from the manager that I had done a good job entertaining his tea party, Gordon gave me £7 as my fee, but I didn't like to accept it all. We agreed on £3 10s. 0d. for me, and £3 10s. 0d. for him as my agent for the day. It meant I could buy something from the seaside to take home for the children.

It was a few days later when Gordon had ended his spell of card magic at the Excelsior and I was back to normal, patrolling the main street of Strensford. A little old lady peered at me very closely, then said in all seriousness, 'By gum, I would never play cards with you!' and walked away.

We learned that Dave Cotterell was a false name for the hotel thief; but in spite of nationwide investigations and searches, he was never traced or identified.

Another thing I discovered through studying the art of magicians was that members of the public can be persuaded to believe things which are not really happening. Disappearing coins, cards and cigarettes are small examples because, of course, they do not actually vanish, they merely seem to do so.

On the bigger stage, some magicians were capable of amazing illusions, even to the extent of cutting a woman in half, walking through a solid wall or disappearing from a closed cabinet. There were times I realized that a study of the illusionist's technique could be useful when trying to detect crime, or at least persuade witnesses to explain precisely what they had seen, heard or otherwise experienced. A personal example occurred when, during part of my police career, I drove twenty miles to work every day. Because there were two routes of exactly the same distance between my home and the police training school where I was then stationed, I used to alternate, selecting first one route and then the other to provide a little variety during my daily journey. Along both routes, I came to recognize other cars as they were heading towards me; each route had its own regular travellers.

Then one day I met one of the women whom I encountered regularly upon one of those routes.

'Oh, I recognize you,' she said. 'We pass each other every morning at the same time and in almost the same place.'

As I chatted to her, I realized she believed that to be true, even though we passed one another no more frequently than every other morning. Had I been a criminal wanting a false alibi, she might have provided one by saying she'd seen me on a particular date when in fact I had not chosen her route. Quite unwittingly, I had created an illusion worthy of the best magician! The witness was convinced I was somewhere I was not.

This equates with the criminal's old trick of deliberately but apparently accidentally spilling a drink or food down someone's clothing, and then offering to pay for the cleaning while obtaining the victim's name and address. Later, if questioned by the police, the criminal would cite that incident as an alibi. If the person with the damaged clothing was interviewed by the police, he or she could recall the incident. The trick, of course, was that the criminal would provide a false date. It often meant the victim could easily recall the incident, but quite often not the exact date. And so a false alibi could be created – another example of an illusion.

Some of our famous fictional detectives, such as Sherlock Holmes, were aware of this propensity for people to be deceived, often unintentionally and often through their own actions or way of life. Perhaps Sherlock's best known example is the dog in the night. In Sir Arthur Conan Doyle's story *Silver Blaze* (1892), a man stole a horse from some stables. Witnesses did not hear the dog bark when the thief arrived and so Sherlock deduced the dog must have known the thief. One can understand the value of this logic when modern detectives ask, 'Did you hear anything suspicious?' Perhaps they should ask, 'Did you hear anything out of the ordinary? Or did you see anything out of the ordinary?' Perhaps they should enquire whether the witnesses did not hear anything they might otherwise have heard or expected to hear? A similar incident occurred when a witness failed to notice routine sounds outside his house.

Many of us are like that – if sounds have persisted over the years, we tend not to notice them.

It is like people who live on rural railway stations: they never hear passing trains, while people living near motorways and airports can block out the sound of moving vehicles or aircraft. Nonetheless, a silence can be just as important – and just as suspicious – as a sound.

In the world of professional magic, an illusionist is a person who does not rely on sleight of hand and I recall one such trick where the magician apparently walked through a solid wall. The illusion was performed before an audience and it began with a party of perhaps a dozen fast-working men in flat caps and overalls placing large sheets of plywood on the stage to prove that the illusionist was not going to rely on hidden trapdoors. In some versions, a large turntable was on the stage so that when the wall was built upon it, it could be revolved to allow the wall, at various states of construction, to be viewed from all angles by the audience. Once the plywood was in position, or the turntable viewed by the audience, the workmen began to build a solid wall either on the plywood floor, or on the turntable.

When the wall was about four feet high, a man-sized windowless cabinet was placed at one side. It was entirely black inside and the door faced the audience; it was opened to show it empty with a solid back and one solid side; the open side adjoined the wall. An identical cabinet was positioned at the other side of the wall. Clearly, they were separated by the solid wooden blocks. It was the magician's task to enter one cabinet and pass through the wall of blocks to emerge from the second.

Once the cabinets were both in position, the magician entered the first cabinet where he could be seen inside by the audience. They had a clear view of him.

He then closed the door but his head and shoulders would remain visible while the wall was under construction. The workmen resumed their frantic wall-building, continuing until it was about six or seven feet high during which time the magician was incarcerated in that first box. The rising blocks totally concealed him. Soon there was a solid complete wall of wooden blocks on view to everyone. When it was finished, there would be a roll of drums, and the magician would apparently walk through the wall to step out of the second cabinet, which he did to great applause.

This illusion had all the hallmarks of being impossible, certainly before the days of television trickery but in fact it was humiliatingly simple. Each of those cabinets had two doors, one at the front and one at the back. The one at the back was unknown to the audience because it looked just like the solid black rear wall of the box. When the audience had peered into the cabinet as the man entered, it looked like a large black sentry box with a solid side, a solid back and a door at the front. The open side of each box abutted the wall of wooden blocks.

When the magician entered the first one he waited until the rising wall concealed him, then put on a cap and set of overalls which were hidden and awaiting him behind a black panel. He then emerged unseen through the back door and joined the other workmen. He actually helped to build the wall. The success of this illusion depended upon the audience acting in accordance with normal human nature. Who among them would try to count those fast-moving workmen? An extra one among them would not be noticed.

As the wall neared completion, the magician would simply slip into the second cabinet via its secret back door, discard and hide his disguise in the specially built place to later emerge after a roll of drums. It is like the language of the American Indians – easy when you know how. This kind of illusion has occasionally been duplicated on sports fields – people have been known not to notice an extra man in the field during a cricket match, or an extra man in the rugger field.

So how can knowledge of the mechanics of this kind of illusion help the police to detect crime? One thing to remember is that this trick was not merely an illusion – there were many conspirators too, all keeping the magician's secret and helping him achieve his goal. Or could he keep his secret even from those stage workmen? Would they know he had joined them for just a short while?

Perhaps the following case might have similarities to that kind of illusion. Every Wednesday, the old market in Strensford came to life with stalls selling all manner of domestic requirements from fish, fruit and vegetables to shoes, rugs and electrical goods. It attracted large numbers of people from the town and surrounding villages, but it also brought in day-trippers and holiday-makers who liked its atmosphere and range of local products. Invariably, market day also attracted what might be termed fringe operators – people who did not hire a stall but who came to sell or show their personal creations, sometimes offering home-made artwork such as jewellery from a tray, or even cakes and buns. Likewise, charity collectors sought donations for a range of worthy causes, such as Red Cross, the Royal National Lifeboat Institution, animal welfare and a host of other charities, local and national.

In short, the marketplace was busy and bustling throughout the day but was seldom a cause for concern to the police, even if the local inns were open for business from morning till night. I have already told the tale of filming in this marketplace, but the following is another yarn.

No one was surprised when a man arrived complete with a large black briefcase, a clipboard, official forms and an orange weatherproof coat bearing, on the back in black letters, a large notice saying, 'Official Survey'. He positioned himself at one of the busy corners and stopped people as they headed towards the market stalls. I chanced to be on duty in the market around half-past ten when it was enjoying one of its periodic busy spells and went across for a chat with him. I always felt it wise to know what was going on.

'Morning, Constable.' He was a well-spoken man in his late thirties, but because of his large all-embracing coat, I could not see whether he was smartly dressed or otherwise. His dark hair was neatly cut and he was clean shaven. Judging by his manner, I guessed he would be smartly dressed – he looked like an official of some kind. He smiled and said, 'I won't quiz you, it's the local customers and visitors that interest me, people who are visiting the market on a regular basis, not officials working here.'

'So what's the survey all about?'

He showed me one of his printed forms which was clipped to his board.

It was headed *Ministry of Transport* and beneath were the words, *The Traffic Signs Regulations and General Directions. 1964, and Pedestrian Crossings ('Push Button Control) Regulations. 1962. National Survey.* Underneath was a blank space and in it for today's survey there was written, in handwriting, the words, 'Strensford Marketplace' and the date. There were spaces for the name and address of those he questioned, and columns for matters such as the age and sex of the person questioned, whether they were disabled, whether they came alone or with family, friends, children, dogs or elderly people, the frequency with which they came to the place being surveyed, in this case Strensford marketplace on market day, the duration of their stay, whether they combined this visit with a trip into the rest of the town, or to have lunch, visit a friend, go shopping or even visit the cinema. There were also columns to tick as an indication of whether the persons questioned had travelled into town by bus, train, car, taxi, pedal cycle, on foot, on a horse or by other means. I noticed that beneath each form was a carbon paper, allowing an instant duplicate to be made.

At the foot of the single-page form I noticed the final question: 'Would a push-button controlled pedestrian crossing, i.e. a panda crossing, be an asset at this point?' There were boxes to tick – Yes, No, Don't know. Panda crossings, as distinct from zebra crossings, were introduced to a few areas in 1962 but they were innovative in that they were operated by pedestrians pressing a button if they wished to stop the traffic and cross the road.

He told me, 'It follows the introduction of panda crossings, Constable. They've not been universally accepted by local authorities, and the public don't seem to have taken to them either. My task is to question local residents who are regular attenders at this market to see whether a panda crossing is needed, or even desirable, probably at the point I am standing at this moment. It's all part of the Ministry's nationwide focus on road safety.'

The place he was stationed was busy, being the main point of entry into the market both for pedestrians and vehicles, and it seemed to me that such a crossing might be beneficial, although I had no knowledge of any statistics of traffic accidents at this point.

'So are you here long?' I asked.

'All day!' he sighed. 'I started at 9.30, and I'll be here until 4.30 this afternoon. Tomorrow, I shall have to summarize and analyse the data I have collected and then on Friday, it's Ashfordly market, Eltering next Monday, more analysis in between times...'

'So does it mean we'll be getting a panda crossing here?'

'Not necessarily. It all depends on the volume of traffic and number of pedestrians using this location, and of course, any relevant accident figures over the past five years. I shall get those later. But the Minister of Transport and his advisers are very much in favour of these crossings; they regard them as beneficial to road safety.'

'Well, I wish you all the best,' I said, and

left him.

As I patrolled the marketplace for half an hour or so I saw him approach several people, mainly women shoppers although there were a few men among his clients. All seemed willing to assist him. I left the market to head for the harbourside to complete a patrol along the quay for an hour or so, and that would be followed by my refreshment break in the police station. My break was scheduled between 1.30 p.m. and 2.15 p.m. the statutory three-quarters of an hour.

Just as I finished and was preparing to resume my patrol, Sergeant Mason came into the rest room. 'Ah, Nick. Glad I caught you. Can you go up to Waterloo Crescent, no. 24, a Mrs Collier? She says someone's broken into her house through the back kitchen window. There's no one in CID at the moment, so check out her story and if you think it's necessary, get Scene of Crime to come out from Divisional Headquarters.'

It took me nearly fifteen minutes to walk to Mrs Collier's house and when I rang the front doorbell, she answered the door in seconds. In her early fifties, she was a plump woman with a round face, one I felt would be cheerful in normal circumstances, but now she looked upset and tearful. I opened the proceedings by introducing myself by name.

'Thank goodness you've come, I don't know what to do, Officer ... why me? Why break in here?'

'When did it happen?'

'Well, I left here about quarter to ten and went into town for coffee with Alice, she's a long-time friend. We did a bit of shopping together and I had a light lunch with her, then got back a few minutes ago to find my kitchen window had been smashed. At first I thought it must be a stone thrown by a child or something like that, then I saw the footprint on the kitchen windowsill and the hole in the glass, then realized I'd been raided. They've taken money Constable, money I'd been saving...'

'Show me,' I requested.

She led me to several places where she had hidden money, including a shoebox in her wardrobe, the inside pocket of an old overcoat she never wore, and a biscuit tin in the kitchen. She did not know the precise amount which had been taken but thought it was in the region of a hundred pounds, all in notes. She had checked her other valuables such as jewellery in her dressing-table drawer, and a few modest antique ornaments in a glass case, but they had not been touched. I told her neither to touch the broken window nor the places from which money had been taken, and not to clean up the footprint on her windowsill until after the Scene of Crime team had concluded their examination – the footprint, left because the intruder had stepped on the soil of her back garden, could be a most useful piece of evidence.

There may be fingerprints in the house too. I suggested she made a pot of tea which we could sip while I wrote down her statement which was required for the crime report; after any kind of shock, a cup of hot sweet tea is a wonderful restorative.

As we compiled the statement, I asked who knew she would be out of the house today.

'I go out regularly, Mr Rhea. I suppose anyone living nearby might know I always get the bus. And Alice and I go out every Wednesday for a spot of lunch and shopping in the market, but I can't think of anyone else who would know the house would be empty. I don't think any of my neighbours would do a thing like this.'

'I'll talk to them anyway,' I said. 'Just to

see if they noticed anything out of the ordinary. Now, can I use your phone to call the office? I want to get Scene of Crime here as soon as possible.'

And so this small but annoying crime was officially registered and my investigation began. My first task was to question her again about anyone who might have known the house was empty, even someone who might have overheard her conversation, perhaps in the street or on the bus, but as I was pressing her to try and recall any likely names or occasions, the telephone rang. She answered.

'It's for you,' she said, passing the handset to me. 'The office.'

I responded and it was the duty constable in the inquiry office. 'Nick,' he said. 'We've had another reported break-in, not far from where you are now .Nelson Street, no. 22, a lady called Alice Davison. Can you go there when you've finished at Mrs Collier's? There's still no one in CID.'

'Right,' I promised. Any news of SOCO?'

'Yes, they're on their way to Mrs Collier's. I'll send them on to Mrs Davison straight afterwards, it looks as if we've got a mini-crimewave.'

'Right,' I said. 'I'll be just a few more

minutes here.'

When I told Mrs Collier, she put her hands to her mouth and said, 'Oh dear, that's Alice, my friend. She was with me until lunchtime. How do these criminals know when we are out? How do they?'

'I wish I knew,' I said honestly. 'I'll go there next, before I start asking the neighbours. There must be a link between the two. Are you sure you didn't say something on the bus? Something to alert an earwigging housebreaker?'

'I can't remember, but you don't recall ordinary conversations, do you? Unless they are about something special or important. But the bus was busy, although I can't remember any suspicious people sitting near us.'

She told me the route number for the bus, and the time she and her friend caught it, and I said I would make inquiries at the depot just in case the conductor had noticed any devious characters on board.

I then asked, 'When you and Alice were shopping, did you give your addresses to the assistants for any reason? To have deliveries made perhaps? Or for an invoice to be sent?'

'No, it wasn't that kind of big shopping expedition. A good deal of our time was

243

spent in the market, we had coffee there, and did a bit of grocery shopping.'

'Did you give your name and address to anyone there? See anyone untrustworthy who might have recognized you?'

'No – oh, except for that man doing the survey about pedestrian crossings.'

'Really?' For some reason I recalled the carbon paper beneath the form on his clipboard. 'What did he ask?'

'He asked if we were local ladies because he did not wish to question anyone who did not live in Strensford. He said it was in connection with a proposed pedestrian crossing near the entrance to the market square, and he wanted only the opinions of people who regularly used that route, either by car or on foot. He said we were the ones who would have to put up with it all day every day.'

'And did he write down your address?'

'Yes, I saw him do it. Then he asked me all sorts of questions and either wrote the answers on his board or ticked boxes. He did the same with Alice. But he was from the Ministry of Transport or somewhere, he wouldn't break into my house!'

'But he did know your address, and because you were talking to him, he did know your house was empty, at least temporarily.'

244

'My husband might have been there!'

'He wasn't though, was he? Did the man ask about him?'

'Yes, he did. I said I was a widow, which I am. And so is Alice.'

As I concluded my questioning of Mrs Collier and walked around the corner to Nelson Street, thoughts of the man taking the survey came to mind. The form I had seen did contain spaces for name, address, age and marital status. One might assume this information was necessary if the value of a panda crossing was being considered but how genuine was that man? He looked real enough as did his forms, but how could he commit these housebreakings if he was in the marketplace all day?

But had he been there all day? After talking to Mrs Davison, I would have to hurry back to the market to see if he was still there.

First, though, I needed to hear her story. The information gleaned from Mrs Davison was almost identical to the experience of her friend. Cash had been taken from various storage places in her house, not as much as Mrs Collier had lost, but a fairly substantial sum of about £40. I rang the office from Mrs Davison's phone and said I had a suspect, but they said yet another house had been broken into this morning. That one had suffered the theft of about £50 and so one of the town constables had been despatched to commence an investigation. I hurried down to the marketplace but it was quarter to five when I arrived, and everyone was packing up after a hectic day. Of the man from the ministry there was no sign. And, of course, I had no address for him! But when I returned to the police station, I could check his authenticity through the Ministry of Transport offices.

One or two stallholders were still around as I strode around the marketplace and when I asked each if they recalled the man from the ministry, all of them did. In fact, he had asked one or two of them what they felt about a panda crossing and when I asked if he had been in position all day, they all confirmed that he had. He'd even eaten his lunch at his post, they said, and the cafe on the corner had taken him a cup of coffee that morning, and a cup of tea in the afternoon. So if he had been there all day, he could not have committed those crimes.

And yet, I told myself he had access to the names and addresses of at least two of the victims, the two I had interviewed.

I hadn't been able to check with the third at this stage but I could not forget the sight of that carbon paper. So did he have an accomplice? If two of them were operating some kind of criminal activity, the sight of a man coming to chat with the man from the ministry would not be unusual – he was chatting to men and women all day. And a colleague collecting forms from him would not be unusual. If he had passed a carbon copy of his forms to that man, or even the entire forms, could he have then committed the crimes? By taking a town service bus to the target premises perhaps? Or walking – in a small town like Strensford the furthest boundaries were only a twenty-minute walk from the marketplace. The more I thought about it, the more convinced I was that the man from the Ministry was behind those crimes, and when I discovered the story of the third victim, it transpired she had also been shopping in the market and town centre during the morning. The constable who interviewed her had not thought to ask whether she had given her name and address to anyone whilst away from home but, none-theless, I felt I had enough evidence to regard the fellow as a prime suspect.

Back at the police station before going off-duty, I presented my theories to Sergeant Mason and he agreed with me. CID had not yet turned up – Strensford's two detectives had been drafted into Scarborough to keep secret observations for a team of building society raiders thought to be targetting the town's offices but he said he would inform the detective sergeant of this development. As I was not due to work in Strensford during the following few days, he suggested I try to establish the credence of the man from the ministry by contacting the local offices.

If they had no knowledge of him, we might have to launch a large-scale search for him and his accessory

Back in Aidensfield, I spoke to Sergeant Craddock and he allowed me time away from routine patrol work to conduct my own inquiries into the mysterious affair. To cut short a long story, the Ministry of Transport had no record of anyone conducting a survey into panda crossings, and if they had wanted that kind of statistical input, it would not have been done in the manner I described. Suitably humbled, I decided to ring Strensford Police to give them the good news. Then I remembered the fellow saying he would be visiting other market towns, including Ashfordly. Was that genuine or was he trying to set up a false trail? Or did he believe he was so competent in the way he committed his crimes, that he would never be traced, or certainly never convicted?

When I rang Strensford, I was connected with Detective Sergeant Readman and updated him.

'Good work, Nick, so what do you suggest?'

'We should set up a sting operation. Get a senior-looking detective, a woman, to visit him and provide details of an address, saying she is out all day if he asks the question. We watch the premises, and if his accomplice then goes to break in, we let him get inside – we need that as proof of his guilt – and arrest him. Once we've got the accomplice under lock and key, we go and lift that man from the ministry and seize his file of forms as evidence.'

'Sounds feasible to me. You say he's expected in Ashfordly tomorrow? It doesn't give much time to set up an operation. If we let him go ahead without arresting him, it might give us more time and more evidence of the pattern of their activities. Then we might be able to set up a similar operation somewhere else.'

'We might not know where else he's going,' I reminded him. 'There's no guarantee he's even going to Ashfordly.'

'True, true. So it's all a bit uncertain but even so you'd still suggest Ashfordly tomorrow?'

'He mentioned it and knew it was on a Friday, but he also mentioned Eltering on Mondays. He might have done that to provide a smokescreen, although we might consider one of the other markets which operate on a Friday – Helmsley, Easingwold, Leyburn, Malton or Stokesley.'

'We can't spare the personnel to cover them all,' he said. 'Not all at the same time, I mean. It's one or nothing at the moment.'

'Well, if he's not at Ashfordly by, say, 10 a.m., then Helmsley's only twenty minutes away…'

'Point taken! All we need look for is a man carrying out a survey, but the real culprit is his accomplice, right? You think ministryman provides the information and miladdo does the breaking?'

'Yes, and he'll have a carbon copy of the target addresses with him.'

'Right, leave it with me, Nick. Instead of having someone sitting and waiting in a target house, we might be able to set up a shadowing operation, but we do need to catch the villain actually inside the house. We can't arrest people for what they might be thinking of doing, we've got to catch him in the act of committing the crime.'

'I think the accomplice picks up his addresses from time to time in the market, so if we kept observations for that transaction to occur, the minute the fellow is out of sight with his target address in his hands, we arrest the ministry-man and let the other chap go ahead, shadowing him all the way ... that way, the accomplice couldn't be warned that his partner had been nicked. We would have some time at our disposal because he wouldn't go back for another few addresses until sometime later.'

'Right. We'll work something out. Leave this with me, and thanks for your input. We could make a good detective out of you!'

The fake man from the Ministry – Jeremy Jardine – was arrested in Helmsley market-place that Friday, having been cunning enough to try and mislead me, and his partner, a well-known housebreaker called Alfred Stanley Marshall, was caught breaking into a house, with the carbon copies of Jeremy's 'forms' in his pocket.

Theirs had been a polished operation, one

which would not cause suspicion to the average bystander or member of the public. After all, how many would associate a man who never left the marketplace with house-breakings occurring in another part of the town whilst he remained on view in the marketplace?

But in my view, the activities of that pair were good proof of the way some of our great illusionists understood the fallibility of human nature.

But it must always be remembered that you can fool some of the people for some of the time, but you can't fool all of the people all of the time.

CHAPTER 7

One of the most remarkable features of Britain's coastline is the lifeboat service, not only because it is staffed by volunteers but also because it is funded entirely by voluntary contributions. I believe it is the only British public service to be financed in this manner (although the modern Yorkshire Air Ambulance service likewise receives no government funding). However, the lifeboat service has no income from taxes or Government funds, and, of course, its record of saving lives at sea is beyond compare. Not long ago, the service relied entirely on volunteers using small rowing boats which were kept on shore ready for emergency launching, but today their work is aided by high-tech motorboats, inflatables and helicopters. Nonetheless, the risks and dangers of the sea remain.

It is rare for police officers to be involved in rescues by lifeboat. During my service on duty in the coastal areas, however, we were quickly made aware of any ongoing rescue attempts, just as the entire population of the town or village was made aware. Without exception, news of a local seaborne drama spread through a small community with bewildering speed, particularly if a local boat was involved, and lots of people would hurry to the harbourside to watch the launch of the lifeboat and cheer its brave crew.

Strensford was no exception. The lifeboat house was on the eastern side of the harbour, a large shed on concrete stilts which stood high above the water so that the lifeboat could be launched whatever the state of the tide, even when it was very high or very low.

Separated by about a hundred yards of water, viewers could stand on the other side of the harbour to watch the launch and although the boat was not accompanied by flashing blue lights and two-tone horns as it swept down the ramp to hit the water with a mighty splash, there was always a tangible sense of drama. Once the lifeboat was heading out to sea, the crowd would move towards the twin piers from where, with binoculars, they might sometimes watch the drama being enacted offshore. At other times, the lifeboat would disappear either over the horizon or behind the cliffs which jutted into the North Sea to obscure views to the north and south. If people were really determined to watch, they might drive up to the cliff tops at either side of the town, or onto one of the nesses from where, in daylight, wonderful panoramic views were obtainable. But wherever the lifeboat went, most of the watchers would remain until it returned from its mission, successful or otherwise. In fact, many of those waiting and watching were relatives or friends of the lifeboat crew members, and sometimes friends and relatives of those on other ships who were in such danger at sea.

Naturally, any patrolling police officer

would join the crowd, inevitably with the intention of being on the spot to act immediately if the occasion arose. Even if the drama was out at sea, the police needed to know what was happening in case any assistance was required from the shore-based emergency services. In addition, there might be fatalities which meant the police would be involved in the procedures and inquiries which followed any deaths, or it might be necessary to provide a police escort to rush an ambulance to hospital with a severely injured casualty.

The lifeboat which was kept in the custom-built house beside Strensford harbour was called *Lucy Hewitt* in honour of a major benefactor to the RNLI. In her will, Mrs Hewitt had left sufficient funds to have this boat specially constructed and it had been brought into service in 1957. She – boats are always feminine – was a self-righting motor-boat with a single 40 horsepower petrol engine capable of seven and a half knots and, during my time at Strensford, was credited with saving more than 300 lives.

The town's earlier boat, the *Kate Winspear*, also named after a benefactor, was one of the last rowing lifeboats to be used by the RNLI, and she had been withdrawn from service in

1957. With a crew of fourteen, ten of whom were oarsmen, she had saved over a hundred lives. At the time of my occasional duties in Strensford, *Kate Winspear*, in immaculate condition, was kept in a former lifeboat house on the western harbourside. Now disused as an operational station, that lifeboat house had been transformed into a modest museum where the pristine *Kate Winspear* was permanently on show along with many artefacts, documents and photographs covering the history and work of the Strensford lifeboats. In addition, there was information about the lifeboat service around the entire British coastline with details of famous and heroic rescues. The museum, staffed by dedicated volunteers, also served as a recruiting base and a means of raising much-needed funds. Its wide doors were always standing open during the day, a major attraction in the tourist season, and there is little doubt that *Kate Winspear* and the rescues she had effected were a constant source of wonder and admiration.

In her retirement, *Kate Winspear* continued to perform a very useful fund-raising service for the RNLI even if she never went to sea. But that peaceful retirement was to be interrupted.

It was a winter's night one January in the mid-1960s and I was undertaking a patrol of the town between 10 p.m. and 6 a.m. It was bitterly cold with a strengthening NNW wind coming off the sea, with sleet and snow forecast. In addition to the anticipated storm conditions, it was expected the rising tide would be higher than normal. That combination of weather conditions was always threatening.

The town's fishing fleet had wisely decided not to go to sea until conditions improved and the harbour staff had earlier warned all pleasure boat users not to venture out of the harbour mouth and to ensure their craft were securely moored. News of the worsening weather quickly penetrated the consciousness of the townspeople; it became the main topic of conversation in pubs, clubs, private houses and even among groups gathered on street corners. It was anticipated that the tide, which was due to reach its peak just after 2 a.m., would be nine or ten feet higher than normal which, driven by a force 9 gale coming off the sea, would produce flooding in some low-lying areas of the town.

Any houses or other buildings standing close to the sea might also be damaged –

windows could be put out by high water, ground-floor rooms flooded and even doors smashed. Cars left out on the streets were also at risk and anyone foolish enough to take a late-night stroll near the water's edge was also in danger.

The twin piers would also become highly dangerous and people would be banned from venturing along them, the fear being they might be swept over the railings and into the raging sea below. Rescue in such circumstances would be almost impossible, particularly in the darkness. The high seas would also batter the cliffs and coastline, spilling onto the coastal roads in massive, powerful waves of water and foam; those roads which skirted the beaches little higher than sea-level were the most at risk and so efforts would be made to prevent traffic using them. Even so, some drivers and pedestrians would ignore the warning signs – they always did. The townspeople were quite accustomed to this kind of drama and tended to take such threats in their stride but for me, it was something quite new and exciting, if more than a little alarming.

As I started my patrol of the streets, none of which was very far from the harbourside, I could hear the roar of the wind out at sea and the ceaseless crashing of waves against the piers and cliffs. It sounded like a different world out there. In the town centre, the wind was strong enough to blow rubbish along the streets, to send dustbin lids clattering into alleys and yards and to compel people to hang onto their hats, but the cluster of buildings beside the harbour provided a great deal of shelter. People who built towns and villages close to the sea were very skilful in providing havens of calm in the most ferocious storms.

Even in the town centre, however, there were flurries of sleet and gusts of powerful wind, with surges of seawater swelling in the harbour to send waves splashing onto the nearby streets.

This sent mini white horses along the carriageways and footpaths, just like a tide washing the beach.

Prior to beginning our patrols, all the duty constables had been provided with details of the forecast, and given orders not to venture close to the water's edge or the harbourside unless some urgent matter demanded attention; we must not put our own lives at risk but at the same time we had to be constantly aware of any incident which might demand the attention of the emergency services.

And then at midnight, there was drama. Somewhat isolated from the centre of things, I had no idea what had caused the alarm or what had happened but as the sleet was threatening to turn into snow, I became aware of people running along the streets towards the harbourside. With no personal radio sets in those days, and without contact with the police station, I could only guess there had been some kind of problem at sea and so I decided to head towards the harbourside, just like everyone else. It seemed as if the entire population was heading that way. I was only some five minutes away from the quayside and instinctively followed the crowd. As I reached the harbour, I realized lights were burning in the lifeboat house and there was a lot of activity both in the lifeboat house and around it. It was clear that the lifeboat was about to be launched on this most dreadful of nights.

The harbour, normally fairly calm, was now like a miniature rough sea with waves being swept in from beyond the ends of the piers. They were rolling in to crash against the harbour walls and fling water into the streets and alleys while tossing lightweight boats around like corks.

So far as I could see in the darkness, none

had slipped their moorings but their plight gave some indication of what might be happening beyond the protection of the harbour. I had to find out and, if necessary, ring the police station from one of the nearby kiosks to provide a situation report. As I moved through the gathering crowds, all of whom stood in safe places, I asked a man, 'Any idea what's going on?'

'Aye,' he said. 'A coaster's engines have packed up. It's gone aground on t'rocks below Blackstone Cliffs. T'lifeboat's going to try and get t'crew off. It won't be easy in this weather, I can tell you, not on them rocks.'

'Thanks.'

I waited until the lifeboat and its crew had been launched, then hurried to the nearest telephone kiosk and rang Strensford Police Station. The night duty office constable answered, and I told him what was happening. Blackstone Cliffs were about a mile south of the harbour entrance, an area noted for shipwrecks down the centuries. Stretching for nearly half a mile out to sea from the base of the cliffs, Blackstone Rocks was the name of a huge area of massive boulders, the size of several football pitches. For most of the time they were visible above the surface of the sea and maritime charts clearly showed them, although at very high tide they could be hidden beneath the waves – especially in the darkness. Untold numbers of ships, often those from foreign countries, had come to grief there, some with a loss of life. Wind and tide conditions could quickly sweep unwary vessels onto the rocks especially if their engines failed, and once a ship was marooned there, it could rarely be refloated.

It was almost inevitable that it was broken up to become a wreck as high seas relentlessly pounded it day after day.

'Thanks, Nick,' he said. 'We've already had a call from the coastguard and the lifeboat's being launched. There's not a lot we can do except wait, but the inspector has ordered that all constables on duty in the town to proceed to the harbourside to keep a watching brief and report any progress or any need for emergency action from onshore.'

'No problem,' I said, and resumed patrol. When I returned to the harbourside, the crowd had swollen considerably with lots of anxious faces waiting in the darkness, the street lights having been extinguished at midnight. Beyond, we could hear the storm raging out to sea, with the wind roaring up the harbour in powerful gusts and the sleet continuing to arrive in sudden chilling flurries. Boats rocked and swung at their moorings as people did not know what to do – in fact there was nothing anyone could do, except for that brave crew aboard the *Lucy Hewitt*. We hoped they knew what they were doing – all we could do was wait.

Fortunately, modern lifeboats were equipped with radio and lights, and although there had been occasions in the past when lifeboats had failed to find stricken ships in the darkness, it was felt among those around me that this helpless coaster would be found. After all, its location was known and it would surely be showing lights even in its present condition.

Nothing happened for about an hour and then there were further signs of urgent activity.

Men began to run along the harbourside, heading towards the piers and I managed to shout at one of them.

'What's happened?'

'*Lucy Hewitt*'s engine's flooded, she's gone aground an' all. That's two of 'em aground on Blackstone Rocks. And their crews.'

'She'll float off, won't she? At high tide? There's an hour to go.'

'We haven't time, we can't wait. We're going to get *Kate Winspear* out of t'museum, she's lighter, she won't get stuck on t'rocks. If she does, we can get her off. But we need men to get her moving, down to the old slipway ... the more the merrier.'

'You've got a crew?'

'Oh, aye, we allus have standby crews, these lads here. And there'll be all the gear in the museum. Oars, torches, loudhailer...'

And so a crowd of eager men, including myself and some bystanders who had overheard our conversation, ran through the driving sleet and spray from crashing waves, heading along the harbourside towards the lifeboat museum. The leader, whose name I never did discover, produced a key for the massive doors of the former lifeboat house and swung them open. As the lights came up, we saw the gleaming old lifeboat in her white and navy blue livery and she was resting on the wheeled undercarriage which had been formerly used to launch her. In her day, a launch meant hauling the under-carriage and its load from this boathouse, then going about fifty yards along the public highway to a narrow slipway which ran down to the beach.

That shipway was almost within the shadow of the west pier.

It had high walls at each side, one being the

retaining wall of the pier and the other forming the foundations of a complex of seaside shops and restaurants, right on the water's edge. Now of course, the tide was in, and it was especially high which meant it was roaring up the slipway and almost reaching dry land but it also meant the boat would hit the water almost as soon as it reached the slipway, thus saving precious time.

Prior to that, its fastenings would be loosened so it would float away from the undercarriage, and then the wheels would be withdrawn and secured until they were needed later to retrieve the boat. We just hoped the storm would allow the launch to take place but these lifeboat men were undaunted by the thought of a few massive waves. And so it was that a motley band of volunteers, with ropes and muscle-power, got the lifeboat moving on its undercarriage. The undercarriage was always kept well greased so that, if required, the boat could be taken outside and placed on the harbourside or bandstand for display on special occasions. Once we had got the wheels turning, it was a fairly simple operation, in spite of the storm, for dozens of men to push and pull the carriage the short distance to the slipway.

When we reached the top, the sea was almost as high as the upper reaches, roaring and splashing and spitting, hurling foam and water high into the air and sending waves washing around our feet. But the lifeboat crew knew precisely what to do. They boarded the old boat in their oilskins, settled in pre-selected rowing positions and picked up the oars which were resting beneath the seats.

When everyone was settled and acquainted with the awesome task ahead, the skipper boarded and gave the command to launch. The undercarriage, now held back by ropes in the hands of local men, was shouldered into position at the top of the slope, and then it began to move downwards towards the waves. As the heavy undercarriage rolled down, still on a firm base but now beneath the waves, the boat floated away and the oarsmen headed into the darkness to begin their terrible task.

I think the worst of the sea probably occurred as giant waves were squeezed into the narrow gulley which formed the walled sides of the shipway because, once *Kate Winspear* had, like a cork, bounced her way from that enclosure into the open sea beyond, she seemed to settle down as the oars flashed in the fading light from the town. We all stood and watched as she headed out to sea, propelled only by man-power. We cheered as she vanished into the darkness with the wind roaring and the sea slapping against the pier walls and the gulley through which the old lifeboat had passed. At the end of each pier there was a small lighthouse which would guide the crew for part of their journey, then their progress might depend on lights from the stricken coaster or *Lucy Hewitt*. Once again, all we could do was wait.

When we returned to the old boathouse, it was surrounded by townspeople with some waiting in the darkness, braving the wind and the sleet, while others were sheltering inside, but there was nothing to see and no one to ask about progress. We stood there, chattering and trying to keep warm and then, after an hour and a half, the boathouse museum's telephone rang.

A man wearing a storm suit bearing the RNLI logo went to answer it. Everyone fell silent as he listened and spoke, then he replaced it.

'That was the coastguard,' he shouted to us all. '*Kate Winspear* has got there, she's taken the crew of the coaster on board, all safe and sound. There's only five of them. And with the tide rising higher than the rocks, they've managed to shift *Lucy Hewitt* off, helped by a bit of muscle-power, good rowing and a long rope! So there we are folks, two lifeboats and three crews, all homeward bound, safe and sound.'

A mighty cheer rose from the crowd.

The man went on. 'The coastguard says the wind has dropped a notch or two, and of course, the tide is turning. It augurs well for a good return trip. I think we should all go to the other lifeboat house to welcome them home. They'll come into the harbour, and now I'd like to lock these doors.'

I had done my bit. In a very minor way I had helped to launch a lifeboat but it was hardly an everyday occurrence for a country constable. It was time to report to the police station. The kettle would be on and I was ready for my sandwiches, but during my break I needed to dry my uniform as best I could. By the time I resumed my patrol, both lifeboats and all three crews had returned safely and I learned that the gallant old lifeboat had suffered some minor damage during the rescue. I wondered who was going to restore *Kate Winspear* to her former glory as a museum piece. Perhaps she should be returned to the museum and retained in her present condition to provide real evidence of her continuing role?

Whatever was decided, the events of that night provided yet another dramatic chapter in the story of our lifeboats.

A combination of high tides and gale force winds was usually a recipe for some of kind of maritime drama, and even places close to the shore of the North Sea can be cruel and dangerous. One of Strensford's more notorious areas was a rocky outcrop situated almost beneath the north side of the west pier. It was a combination of large boulders, seaweed and deep pools.

As the twin piers stretched out to sea, both were shaped like a pair of pincers or even a couple of bananas lying face to face with a gap in between. Where the piers met the sea, the gap was quite narrow but as they extended towards the harbour, that gap widened considerably, and then as the harbour was approached, the gap became narrower again. That shape, like these two brackets ( ), provided a large, almost circular pool of calm water, a refuge for seagoing vessels. Midway along the west pier, at what might be termed its elbow or fingerjoint, there was that large bed of rocks, all below the outer edge of the pier, i.e. its northern side. At low tide, they were fully exposed and children played among them, exploring the many remaining, and now shallower, pools for pretty pebbles, shells and crabs but when the tide roared in, those rocks were completely covered with up to fifteen feet of choppy water which, due to the effect of strong undercurrents, made it dangerous to either swim, paddle or even use small dinghies or other craft. On account of unseen currents, the area was equally dangerous when the tide was ebbing.

On the pier directly above the rocks, were large red noticeboards warning people of the danger below – some foolhardy types were known to dive from the pier when the high tide covered the rocks, a fine way of breaking one's neck or spine. Few realized the additional danger from powerful currents moving beneath the sea which, at times of little wind, could be deceptively calm on the surface. One particularly dangerous time was during spring tides. Contrary to popular belief these are not tides which occur during the spring, but those which rise higher than normal. They tend to appear just after a new or full moon, and the water rises higher than normal because the gravitational power of both the sun and the moon acts in a direct line. Neap tides are the opposite – they attain the least rise and fall at or near the first and last quarters of the moon.

The local people and indeed regular visitors were acutely aware of those dangerous rocks and the effects of the tides and currents around them; for that reason, they were one of the places which attracted would-be suicides. Working in a popular seaside resort made police officers aware of the fact that some people came to the seaside quite deliberately to end their lives, sometimes travelling considerable distances to do so. The reason for this odd form of migration was never known although guesses were frequently made – it was thought that some wanted to end their days in a place they loved, or where they had experienced happy childhood or holiday memories or had enjoyed romantic liaisons.

Whatever the reason, potential suicides would come to seaside resorts such as Strensford to leap off the cliffs, drown themselves at sea, shoot themselves in caves on the beach, gas themselves in cars, slash their throats with razors or hang themselves from trees in nearby woods. There were other bizarre forms of death along with some who never succeeded. For example, it was not uncommon for some to make repeated attempts to drown themselves, their attempts always frustrated through being rescued by well-meaning souls. One man stabbed himself to death in a boarding house with a pair of scissors, inflicting more than seventy wounds before he finally achieved his wish. That smacks of determination and persistence, or a blunt pair of scissors.

It was this peculiarity of human nature which made the rocky pool below the west pier so attractive to suicides. The authorities could do little to prevent people leaping off. They did maintain the necessary warning signs and placed lifebelts in strategic locations (although some were thrown into the sea by vandals), and from time to time the dangers of that pool were highlighted by someone dying there. Even if those warnings deterred sane and sensible people, it could be argued that its dangerous reputation attracted those who wanted to end their earthly existence. The town's police officers were aware of the magnetic effect those rocks exerted upon disturbed people and would make regular patrols to look out for those who might be contemplating a final leap.

Some would stand sullenly over the rocks, peering down into the water for ages before making that dreadful decision to jump.

In a lot of cases they were spotted by the police or harbourside officials and pers-uaded to abandon their attempt. Some went away never to return; others returned with more determination. By contrast, some had been seen to run purposefully towards the railings, climb over and plunge thirty or forty feet into the water almost before anyone noticed them. In some cases their bodies were found and retrieved very quickly while at other times recovery might take days or weeks – and some were lost for ever. Such is the mystery and power of the sea.

It was no surprise, therefore, that a man called Stanley William Carr, a 66-year-old retired postal worker from Wakefield, decided to commit suicide in Strensford. He arrived on a dull and rainy day in early November and found bed-and-breakfast accommodation very easily because it was not the holiday season. Mr Carr settled in to his lodgings quite well although he signed the register as Mr G.D. Wilkinson with a fake address. It was later learned he had told the landlady he had come alone for a quiet break, and that his family might drive over one day later in the week, perhaps to take him out for lunch or even to stay for a few days. He told her he would send his wife a postcard saying where he was staying, and that she might come along too.

What nobody knew at the time of his arrival was that Mr Carr had murdered his wife, Betty. He had viciously attacked her with an axe, and had taken her body in his car to a remote quarry in the Yorkshire Dales where he had dumped her over the lofty edge of a work-face.

He had returned home, cleaned the house as best he could while paying particular attention to the bloodstains, and he'd then decided to go away. He had told his neighbours that he and Betty were going to Scarborough for a short holiday before the winter set in, and so he had left Wakefield in his car. At that time, and indeed when he arrived in Strensford, no one knew his wife lay dead in a far-off quarry. Consequently no one had any cause to worry about her. The neighbours thought the quiet couple had simply gone away for a nice romantic autumnal break. Stanley William, who had a youthful criminal record for violence, rape and various other crimes like housebreaking, burglary and sacrilege, knew it was inevitable that his wife's body would be found and identified, and because he had a serious heart condition he had decided to end his own miserable life.

He had gone straight during the last thirty years of his life, working diligently in a local factory and he had never used violence on anyone, not even on Betty and so the couple were regarded as a thoroughly decent pair. Indeed, they were and so the awful manner of Betty's death was a great puzzle. What had gone wrong was never known; no one knew why he had suddenly done such a thing. However, having experienced prison as a young man, Stanley William had no wish to spend the rest of his days locked away somewhere; he was too old to go on the run and so he had decided to end it all in Strensford where, in fact, he had spent a happy honeymoon. Of course, neither the landlady nor the Strensford Police had any idea of his background, both past and present, prior to these events, nor indeed did anyone realize he was in the town.

After a couple of days in his lodgings, enjoying the hearty breakfasts and comfortable bed, Stanley William decided it was time to bring this sorry saga to its conclusion. He had studied the times of high tides, he knew Strensford very well having been a regular visitor since his honeymoon, he was a non-swimmer and he was very calm and determined, knowing precisely what he was going to do. He had read somewhere that drowning was a wonderful way to die, like going to sleep in the midst of a wonderful dream. His intentions were given a swift boost because, when he read the *Yorkshire Post* that morning, he saw that the body of a woman, identified by her sister as Elizabeth Carr, had been found in the quarry and that foul play was suspected. The report added that the West Riding Police were anxious to trace her husband, Stanley William Carr, who had left the family home, the neighbours saying he'd said he and his wife were going to Scarborough.

At this stage, it had become known that Mrs Carr had not gone to Scarborough, so where had Mr Carr gone? According to the police circular which arrived in Strensford Police Station, it was not yet known whether Mr Carr had committed the crime, or whether someone else was responsible although there was no sign of a break-in at the family home, and an attempt had been made to clean up the blood in the bedroom, droplets of which had already been identified as coming from Mrs Carr's blood group. Clearly Mr Carr had a lot of questions to answer, and the police circular contained a black-and-white photograph of him, obtained from the family home rather than old police files, along with a detailed physical description of him and his motor vehicle.

As the police search was intensifying, with inquiries spreading to Scarborough and other places which Mr Carr was known to have loved, Stanley William was already on his way to Strensford Pier. He had left his car outside the lodging house, heading into town with his destination grimly determined. By chance, I was on duty in Strensford at the time, and the pier was part of my beat.

Stanley William was not the sort of man who would be noticed in a crowd. He was almost invisible among other people, being quiet and polite, and his clothing did nothing to make him prominent. He could have been any middle-aged man going for a stroll. That morning, around eleven, he was heading for the pier clad in a brown trilby and an anonymous fawn raincoat beneath which was a dark tan sports jacket, a pair of pale tan cavalry twill trousers and brown shoes, all rather worn.

Although the town was not very busy people were in the streets, some going about their business, some shopping, some taking late holidays and others enjoying a brisk walk during their lunch break. No one took any notice of the rather stocky, middle-aged man who looked neither to the right or to the left. He walked with an almost dogged determination to reach some distant point, although he was not rushing. To reach the danger point, he had to descend from the higher part of the town where his lodgings were based and negotiate a long flight of steps which took him down to the harbour-side, not far from the lifeboat museum. Although I was not aware of his presence, he must have walked past the museum whilst I was chatting to one of the charming lady volunteers and admiring the *Kate Winspear*.

Following its recent dramatic outing, the wonderful old lifeboat had been cleaned and returned to its indoor berth during the proceeding months, some damage still evident as the authorities considered whether or not to repair it. The museum was open to take advantage of the lifeboat's recently-found fame.

From there, Mr Carr would have to walk

about 150 yards, half of which was along the final approach to the pier. The danger point was about seventy-five yards along the pier. It was high tide at that time, with extra water being generated by a spring tide. There was also a gusty wind, by no means gale force but considerably stronger than a mere sea breeze. The sea was described as choppy which meant the area near the rocks was covered with deep, turbulent waters beneath which were dangerous and strong currents. It was they, rather than the waves, which were the problem.

Although it was a November day it was fine and quite mild with a constant procession of people, many on lunch break, heading down the pier for a sight of the choppy waves and to feel the power of those strong winds coming off the salty sea. It made the cheeks tingle and provided a real sense of well-being. Among the people walking towards the pier was a quiet and very gentle man who owned a bookshop in town. His name was Edward Midgley. He was forty years old with two little girls and a lovely wife. His bookshop was successful and in his spare time he worked for various charities, including the RNLI.

What happened next is a matter for conjecture but the following may be a reasonably accurate account.

I was suddenly aware of a commotion and a woman screaming along the pier so I ran out of the lifeboat museum to see other people running towards the railings which bore the warning signs about the dangers of the rocks below. As I approached, I sensed that someone had climbed over the rails and dropped into the raging waters and I was in time to see Edward Midgley racing towards the rails. He first headed towards a small shelter which should have contained a lifebelt, but it was missing, doubtless thrown away by vandals and so, without hesitating, Midgley climbed onto the rails and launched himself into the water many feet below. There is little doubt he could see Carr thrashing about in his final moments, throwing up his arms as the water did its best to drag him down but I think Carr's clothes, especially the air trapped in his raincoat, helped keep him afloat, at least for a short while. I had not reached the rails by that stage but was aware of another man running with a lifebelt which he had found in a nearby shelter. The man, whose name I did not know, was about thirty and, as he ran, he slipped the lifebelt over his head and shoulders, and held it beneath his arms. Then he climbed onto the rails and leapt in the sea, accompanied by more screams from a lone woman. The lifebelt would keep him afloat, and it was in the ideal position on his body, keeping his head out of the water.

When I arrived at the rails, I saw only two men in the sea. One was the newcomer floating and bouncing on the waves in the security of his lifebelt, trying to reach a second man; the second man was middle-aged and his raincoat was ballooning upon the water to keep him afloat.

The newcomer seized the middle-aged man and began to propel him towards the shore, a difficult task because the fellow seemed to be objecting by shouting and flapping his arms. Of Edward Midgley there was no sign. I was sure I had seen him leap into the cauldron and wondered if he was clinging to one of the ladders on the pier wall. Where had he gone? Indeed, had he jumped? Had I been mistaken? Others who had witnessed the drama said Midgley was somewhere down there but there was no sign of him.

Someone ran to commandeer a small rowing boat which was lying on the beach but there was no point in anyone else leaping into the water, with or without a lifebelt, simply because no one knew what had happened to Edward Midgley, or where he was. Besides, a boat was already on the way. Searching in those conditions was impossible; for anyone else to jump in would create too high a risk because the man in the raincoat was steadily nearing the beach with his rescuer behind, the lifebelt supporting both as the little boat grew nearer.

By the time Carr and his rescuer came ashore, an ambulance had arrived, along with more police officers, and both men were placed inside and whisked up to Strensford Cottage Hospital. A police officer went in the ambulance because I explained I thought Carr, whose name I did not then know, had tried to commit suicide. It was only in the hospital, when his pockets were searched because he refused to reveal his identity or address, that his real name became known. His driving licence was in his wallet – I am sure he thought it would disappear along with his body.

Once his name was known, it was realized we had custody of an alleged murderer.

The unknown man, whose name turned out to be Leslie Ingram, a local bartender, had therefore rescued a person who was later convicted of the murder of his wife.

Edward Midgley's body was found three days later, having drowned in his unsuccessful rescue attempt. In recognition of his bravery he received a posthumous award from the Royal Humane Society and his wife took over the running of his bookshop.

Leslie Ingram also received a medal but he never recovered from the fact he had saved a murderer and allowed a brave family-man to die. He later joined a Benedictine monastery.

CHAPTER 8

Night duty, even in a small town like Strensford, was a revelation. When I was a child and later a pimply youth growing up in the remoteness of the North Riding moorlands, I thought most people went to bed at night, or stayed indoors playing cards or were sometimes really daring and outrageous as they partied into the early hours. Even the Saturday night dances in our village hall ended at 11.45 p.m., this being a provision of the Sunday Observance Act of 1780 which was still powerfully in force during the

1960s. It stipulated that any house, room or other place to which the public were admitted upon payment would be deemed a disorderly house if it opened on a Sunday. Our village elders had no wish for the village hall to be declared a disorderly house which meant our village dances had to end before midnight on Saturday and I believe a similar rule applied to fish-and-chip shops. I can remember an old sergeant of mine checking them all to ensure they were shut before the witching hour of midnight. Later clubs were different and could stay open after midnight on a Saturday because they were not open to the public – their entry was restricted to members.

In my youthful and very rustic world, people such as farmers and agricultural workers climbed out of bed before dawn which meant they had to be in bed very early if they wanted a good night's sleep. The milk, post and newspapers were delivered early too and a lot of small businesses such as builders, blacksmiths, garages and shops started work at either 7.30 a.m. or 8 a.m. I think it is fair to say that most rural workers began their day before dawn, with few working throughout the night.

Of course, some were called out at night in

emergencies, such as the local constable, ambulance driver, fireman, doctor, district nurse or even the parish priest or vicar. Even in my blissful rustic ignorance, I knew that some people in towns worked throughout the night, such as hospital nurses, doctors, ambulance drivers and police officers, but I knew firemen slept in the fire station whilst on night duty. As I grew older, I was also increasingly aware that places of entertainment like nightclubs were open until the small hours with staff and patrons both active during the hours of darkness. But I did not know what occurred in such mysterious places.

Until I joined the police service, however, I had no idea so many other people were active around the streets of our local towns during those late-night hours, or to be precise, the early hours of the morning. They were not criminals; many were carrying out some kind of work or perhaps they were travelling to and from work but in addition there were some who could not sleep and went out for a walk and a breath of fresh air in the hope it would help them get a few hours' rest. And, of course, there were burglars, thieves and other criminals to consider. There was a widespread belief that criminals operated under the cover of darkness which was why police officers patrolled the streets throughout those hours. The odd thing was that I never saw any statistics to prove that theory – it seemed to be a gut feeling among police officers, probably stemming from Victorian times. Some Victorian statutes had created criminal offences which could only be committed at night, e.g. being found at night with one's face blackened or disguised with intent to commit a felony or being armed with an offensive weapon or housebreaking implement by night.

For most purposes, 'night' was the time between 9 p.m. and 6 a.m. and it was also an offence to be or loiter in any highway yard or other place during the night either with the intent to commit a felony or having committed one. Burglary was an offence which could only be committed between the hours of 9 p.m. and 6 a.m., and only by breaking into dwelling houses. Breaking into shops, offices and others buildings was not then classified as burglary whatever time of day it occurred. Because the law considered a man's home to be his castle and somewhere to be safe and secure at all times, especially at night, burglary carried a higher penalty than housebreaking. That was its daytime equivalent although there was a subsidiary offence which said a police constable could arrest anyone found by night in any building with intent to commit a felony therein. As young constables, we had to learn the provision of the so-called night misdemeanours and, of course, there were minor night-time offences such as poaching, drinking alcohol after hours, riding bikes without lights or failing to keep dogs under control at night during lambing time.

The night-time hours were therefore of some importance to young constables but, as I matured, I discovered there was little practical distinction between night and day in busy places like London, Birmingham and Manchester because the streets were brightly illuminated during the whole period of darkness. With street lamps burning all night, few townspeople ever saw the stars or heard the hoot of an owl or the stirring of cows in their fields, and there were people and vehicles on the move the whole time.

Usually of course, that practice applied to the town or city centres rather than suburbia; indeed, the suburbs could be as quiet as our villages with very little night time activity. In town centres, taxis carried out their final trips of the night even as some early workers were beginning their new day. I knew for example, that market traders often started work at 4 a.m. just as fruit-shop owners went to Hull docks at that time to collect their stock for the day; bakers also began at 3 a.m. In Strensford, the fishermen would often put to sea at 2 a.m. or 3 a.m.; people who worked in hotels were early starters and it was surprising how many workers began their day at 6 a.m. or perhaps 7 a.m.: street cleaners, dustmen, newsagents, milkmen, post office workers, harbourside officials, bus and train crews and others all began their day's work before most office staff or teachers had struggled out of bed.

It follows that while performing night duty as a police officer one gains a deeper insight into the non-stop activities of even the smallest community. I remember when I first patrolled the remote countryside around Aidensfield. Sergeant Blaketon once told me that whenever I drove through a village, there would always be a light burning in at least one of the houses. He said there was always someone who was up and about during the night, no matter how small the community and he added that this knowledge was useful when trying to find witnesses to any illegal activity which might have occurred. Most of the time, someone would see or hear something, even if at that moment, they did not appreciate its significance. If a crime occurred and witnesses were sought, it was the police officer's job to find that person, and that often involved knocking on lots of doors.

It is true that witnesses were more likely to recall something which occurred at night when things were supposed to be quiet and peaceful; whatever occurred, however insignificant, the fact it happened at night was frequently sufficient to draw attention to it. Nonetheless, there were people who wandered abroad during the night with absolutely no criminal intent.

I recall one dark and dull November morning when I was completing a period of night duty in Strensford. It was around 5 a.m. and it was bitterly cold. There was a little light from the reflected glow of lights elsewhere in town, but most of my beat was concealed in the darkness and shadows; the sky was also beginning to lighten just a fraction which meant I could patrol without using my torch the whole time. There was a strong breeze coming off the sea and it was enough to send shivers down my spine each time I left a sheltered place to peep round a street corner into the chill wind. It seemed sensible to spend as much time as possible in deep doorways and down alleys which provided shelter from that icy blast.

It was while in such an alley that I became aware of someone hurrying past the entrance about twenty yards away. There was no torchlight from him; it was just the dim image of someone in a rush. I went to the entrance and peered out, looking up and down the street, but saw no one. He'd vanished. A criminal on the run? Hurrying home after committing a burglary perhaps? I had to investigate. As I crept along the street, trying to be as silent and as invisible as possible, I heard a knocking sound but the layout of the street and its houses, many of which lay along deep, narrow alleys, made it difficult to identify the direction from which the sound came.

But it was definitely a loud knocking – someone trying to smash down a door? I waited in a doorway hiding in the darkness and listening, trying to gauge the direction from which it came whilst keeping observations for the man I'd seen earlier. And I dare not use my torch in case it caused the culprit to make a dash for freedom before I caught him.

Then the knocks became a solid hammering and I thought I heard the sound of shouting before someone burst out of an alley about a hundred yards ahead of me. It was a young man in dark clothing but the low glow from the sleeping town was insufficient to clarify his features. And he was running. Had I disturbed a burglar in the act of attempting a break-in? I thought I had and so set off in pursuit. I tried to conceal my presence in the many shadows of the street and to run quietly because I wanted to surprise the villain before he had a chance to vanish among the labyrinth of alleys and passages which are such a feature of Strensford. He would know them far better than I; among that rabbit-warren of narrow lanes he could lose me in seconds. I considered it necessary to get as close as possible before I announced my presence and detained him. Surprise was always beneficial in these circumstances, and it was not difficult for me to conceal my presence in the darkness.

But then he vanished again. I halted, partly to regain my breath and partly to listen for sounds of his next attempt. Most of the houses and shops in this part of town had rear doors which were extremely vulnerable to burglars and shop-breakers, not only due to their flimsy construction and lack of solid locks but also because they were in deep shadows and out of sight from the main thoroughfares.

Furthermore, the network of alleys and passages was linked by others to provide a veritable network of routes in which any local person could quickly lose or out-distance a pursuer. As I stood panting as lightly as I could, I heard more knocking. I thought I had gauged its location and set off again, trotting in the dark shadows with my ears straining to catch every sound. But I had lost my target. He had disappeared somewhere within that network of alleys and I could not hear him, but I continued along the main street, following my instinct. I thought he must be working from one end to the other, using the rear entrances of houses and cottages for his attacks and I reckoned he must emerge onto the main street sooner or later. Then I would see him – and arrest him!

As I approached the entrance to yet another dark alley I heard more knocking and a shout, then almost immediately heard running feet heading towards me. I halted on the main street, close to the entrance to the alley, concealed myself in the shadows and drew my truncheon, just in case there was any kind of trouble. The fact I needed one hand for the truncheon meant I could not use my torch – I needed at least one hand to grab him! At this stage, I could not see my target and did not want him to see me. Then I could hear him pounding towards me, his feet slapping the stones and I knew I had to grab him the moment he bolted from the alley. I reckoned the element of surprise and the cover of darkness would give me the benefit; there was some faint light however, just enough for me to react.

Moments later, the youth bolted out of the narrow entrance and I stepped forward shouting, 'Police, halt!' and seized his arm.

He began to struggle and shout, and in the turmoil he fell over and I landed on top of him. I could not let him struggle free and escape; that would be dreadful, but if he got into those alleys, I'd never find him. And I had no idea who he was.

'Get up!' I ordered. 'Police ... you're under arrest.'

'You what?'

'I said get up, you're under arrest.'

He stood up and stared at me in the gloom, my eyes being well adjusted to the darkness and the meagre light. His pale face showed signs of fear and concern as he brushed his clothes with his hands.

'Arrest? What have I done?'

'Attempted burglary. I heard you trying to smash those doors down.'

'Smash what doors down?'

'In the alleys behind us, two occasions. You were scared off by the householder, I could hear the shouts. And now this one...'

'Don't be daft, officer! I'm not a burglar. You can ask those fellers I knocked at... I'm a knocker-up.'

'A knocker-up? What do you mean? I thought they went out with Charles Dickens.'

'Who's he?'

'Look, what do you mean, knocker-up?'

'It's for those blokes who work at ICI. They have to catch the company bus at six and a lot of 'em have trouble getting out of bed, especially after a night in the pub. So I have to go round knocking them up. That's what I'm doing, and if we stay here much longer, some are going to be late and then there'll be hell on. The bus won't wait and if they don't clock on, they lose money. I have to knock on their doors until a light comes on or until they shout to say they're awake ... I shout at them and they shout back ... that's what the shouting was.'

Quite literally he had taken the wind out

of my sails and, for a moment or two, I was at a loss as to what to do next. Should I believe him or not? Certainly I knew about the fleet of buses which set off early to take workers to ICI on Teesside but I had no idea they employed a knocker-up.

I was still suspicious and so I said, 'Take me to the last man you knocked up, the one down this passage.'

'Look, officer, I know it looks bad for me but I am telling the truth. I have to get round all this lot before half past five...' and he pulled a sheet of paper from one pocket and a torch from another. He shone the torch on a list of names and addresses. 'I've got to go, I'm running late, you've got to let me go to knock them out of bed, otherwise there'll be hell on.'

'Why are you late?'

'I slept in!'

'You, the knocker-up, slept in?'

'Yeh, my mum had to wake me up.'

'So how did your mum come to be awake at this time of day?'

'She has to wake dad up.'

'He's an early starter, is he?'

'Yes, he's one of the bus drivers.'

'Right,' I said. 'Take me to the man down this passage, you come with me, I just want to verify your story.'

When we got to the little cottage, the kitchen light was on and through the uncurtained window we could see a man sitting at the table, eating his breakfast. On the way there, I had learned the lad's name was Jim Gibson and so I knocked on the door. The man did not budge from his meal, but merely shouted, 'All right, all right, I'm up, Jim.'

That was good enough for me. I apologized to Jim for my treatment but he said he understood, although he was now running later than ever. He had several more clients to knock up before the bus departed and was bothered that he might not get round them all in time.

'Give me some names,' I offered. 'I'm on duty until six, I can knock some up for you.'

'Would you?' he sounded most relieved. 'You've got to wait till a light comes on, and you've got to make sure they shout back when you shout at them. That's important, it tells me they've heard me.'

And so it was that I toured some of those alleys and side streets, hammering on eight or nine doors and shouting up at first-floor windows, 'Time to get up', until the inhabitant responded.

I managed to get round them all before

5.30, but I've often wondered if any of those workers realized they'd been knocked out of bed by a policeman. And then, of course, I wondered what their neighbours would have thought about the commotion, especially if they'd looked into the street. That's assuming I might have roused the neighbours too – unless, of course, like so many townspeople, they studiously ignored what was happening next door.

On another occasion, I was undertaking a night patrol in Strensford with my beat including the town centre, the harbourside and the marketplace. It was summer with a warm breeze blowing off the land to make the experience very enjoyable. There was very little happening – the clubs had closed, late-night holidaymakers had returned to their lodgings or holiday cottages and, apart from the early-morning workers, there was very little activity. I was standing at the end of the bridge which spans the harbour, watching the boats and seeing the light of the night sky shimmering on the water, when I noticed a middle-aged woman heading my way. I glanced at my watch – it was 3.30 a.m. and I thought she was looking for me. She seemed to be heading straight for me as she stared in my direction. I made no move then she suddenly veered away and turned along the quayside, walking steadily with a hand outstretched to touch the harbour rail. Then she strode purposefully along the side of the quay heading for the pier which was at least five minutes' walk away. There was no one else around, and she did not have a dog with her.

She seemed in no hurry and I guessed she might be someone unable to sleep, someone wanting some fresh air and exercise. I watched her until she was about two hundred yards ahead and then followed – this was part of my beat and the route would take me past the bandstand which was close to the start of the long walk down the pier. I did not want to alarm her by making her believe I was following her, but I must admit I was curious. As I watched, it dawned on me that she was not walking normally – every so often, she would reach out her right hand to touch the harbour rail, as if seeking solace or reassurance from its presence.

I began to wonder if she was sleepwalking. Another factor which led me to consider that possibility was that, at times, I thought her strides were hesitant almost as if she might be under the influence of alcohol, but she negotiated a row of closed whelk stalls, a deserted ice-cream kiosk, some empty herring boxes, a pile of lobster pots, a parked fish van and various other remnants of the fishing industry which were always left on the harbourside overnight.

As I watched, I decided I should keep her within my sight at all times and I began to wonder if she was aware of my presence even though I was a long way behind and walking silently in my crêpe-soled boots. I saw her give the bandstand a wide berth and then she began her trek down the pier. For the first half of that pier extension, its base was solid concrete with high railings at either side, and rows of benches down the centre. She selected the right-hand side and after reducing the speed of her walk just a fraction to touch one of the rails, she increased her pace and strode purposefully towards the distant end, some quarter of a mile out to sea.

Midway along, however, there was a flight of stone steps, set at an angle where the pier changed direction. The pier's shape was rather like a bent banana or boomerang, and from the top of those steps, its base comprised thick wooden planks with inch-wide gaps in between. Railings extended right to the end and a further circular set enclosed the small lighthouse which stood on the very end of the pier; this far out to sea, of course, the wind was more powerful and the sound of the waves crashing beneath those planks was loud and everlasting. If she was sleepwalking, would she wake up or would she cope with what lay ahead?

I continued to follow her, partly out of curiosity but also because I was concerned for her safety. I hoped she did not intend leaping off the pier to commit suicide – such things did happen here. When she reached the end of the pier, however, she halted and gazed out to sea as the breeze, sea-spray and waves played out their roles around her, and then as I halted behind her, remaining at what I considered to be a sensible distance, she turned around to face me, and then leaned with her back on the rails, facing inland. If she was awake, she would surely see me standing there like a dimwit, watching her. But she made no sign of seeing me. I could have been invisible. I decided she must be sleepwalking.

I had been given to understand, in a first-aid lecture some time earlier, that it was dangerous to wake up a somnambulist, the belief being that the shock of waking in some strange place could induce severe shock or at the worst, cause death. Other lecturers had told us that it was extremely difficult to rouse anyone who was sleepwalking and if we encountered such a person during our patrols, the wisest thing was to guide them gently home. Most sleepwalked within the boundaries of their own homes and returned to their beds unaware of their adventure, but some did venture outside; indeed, there were tales of some driving cars whilst asleep. We were advised that those who went out of the house would eventually find their own way back without waking up, consequently the wisest action was not to try and rouse them, but to accompany them wherever they went to ensure their safety. That is what I decided to do in this case.

I waited for her to move whilst making no attempt to rouse her. She was about fifty-five, I estimated, a sturdily built woman with dark brown hair. She was wearing sensible flat shoes and a light raincoat but no hat or gloves. I did not recognize her and had no idea whether she was a local resident or a holidaymaker, although even in her sleep she did appear to know her way around town – and even around the wealth of obstacles on her walk down the pier. Then she began to walk the way she had come, retracing her steps along the pier and back into town. I stood very still, not wishing to make a sound, and this time she moved across to the other side of the pier, once again the right hand side in the direction she was heading. I waited until she had passed me and then turned around to follow. As I did so, my boots made a slight squeaking sound on the timber.

'Hello,' she said, coming to a halt without turning to look at me. 'Is anyone there?'

I paused, not really knowing how to respond, but then said, 'Yes, I am a policeman, PC Rhea from Aidensfield. I'm doing a relief tour of duty here.'

'Ah,' she said. 'Then you will not know me?'

'No,' I had to admit, now realizing she was not sleep-walking. 'I saw you heading down the pier. I thought you were sleepwalking.'

'So you decided to keep an eye on me?'

'Yes,' I said. 'I didn't want you to come to any harm.'

'That is very kind of you, and I appreciate your concern. But I am not sleepwalking, PC Rhea. I am blind.'

'Oh, I'm sorry.'

'Don't be sorry. I must not feel sorry for

myself; I must cope. I went blind late in life, not many months ago in fact and now I must find my way around town all over again, the town I've known since childhood. I am practising, you see, practising walking around the town without my white stick and without my eyes. That's why I come out at night – night and day are the same to me now but at night there is no traffic and there is no one on the streets for me to bump into. Your colleagues – the ones who are stationed here – all know me, they are quite used to seeing me around the place, practising my walks. I'm Helen Lister, by the way,' and she held out her hand for me to shake.

I took it and shook it, saying I was privileged to meet her. As we walked back along the pier together, she told me about her life and I told her about mine and my family back in Aidensfield, and then we reached the bandstand.

'I have to go along Whitby Road and Gower Street now, that's my route,' I said. 'I'm heading for a telephone kiosk on the corner of Western Avenue where I have to make a point.'

'Well, as you are a stranger in town, let me show you the way,' she offered.

And so she did.

I recall another curious incident during an overnight patrol in Strensford. The first half of my tour of duty had been completed without anything of interest happening and then, after my 45-minute refreshment break in the police station, I continued my quiet beat.

Prior to commencing that shift, however, all night duty officers had been warned of a spate of burglaries in flats above shop premises in and around the town centre. Burglary could only be committed in a dwelling house but a flat, even one above a shop, was classed as a private dwelling. The law governing those crimes, often called 'breaking offences', was changed in 1968, when all offences of breaking into premises were re-classified as burglary

In the Strensford case, it was felt the culprit was a local person because he seemed to know when and where he could operate without being caught or seen. He was targetting flats situated above shops, even those along main thoroughfares, apparently knowing the shop beneath would be deserted during the night. He never broke into the shops and was adept at finding flats whose occupants were absent, either on holiday or because the flat was only used by tenants during holiday periods.

The burglar also seemed to know that many of those flats were not used by the owner of the shop beneath – they were let as an additional means of earning money and so the shopkeeper was not necessarily the keyholder or occupier which meant they were rarely concerned with, or interested in, what occurred to the flat. This often meant the break-in was not discovered until some considerable time after it had occurred, thus giving the thief time to dispose of his ill-gotten goods.

Our local burglar tended to attack the premises from the rear where it was dark and away from the sight of passers-by. He often used a ladder to gain entry. But sometimes climbed the fire escape if there was one, although several flats had been daringly entered from the front, i.e. by climbing a ladder, sometimes in full view of anyone who might have come along the street. Somehow the burglar dodged anyone who might be using the street in question – there were plenty of unlit places he could hide, with or without his ladder. The property stolen was usually something small and portable, like a radio, camera, piece of glassware or a ceramic, things which could be sold for cash and not easily identified. If there was any money on the premises he was skilled in finding it, although temporarily empty flats did not usually contain spare cash. However, judging by the searches he made under mattresses, in cupboards and drawers and even in lofts, it was evident that cash was his main target, his other trophies being substitutes for easy money.

Armed with this knowledge, therefore, I commenced the second half of my patrol, my beat being no. 6 beat which was out of the town centre.

It covered a rather smart area of the town with two shopping arcades, a few hotels, a garage or two and lots of nice houses, many detached in long tree-lined avenues. It was about 3.30 a.m. when I turned towards one of the shopping arcades, my purpose being to shake hands with the door knobs of the shops, both at the front and rear, to ensure they had been secured. That was one of our nightly chores; if we found a shop or other premises insecure, we would knock up the keyholder and get him or her to get out of bed to carry out a check to see whether or not anything had been stolen.

One row of shops on my beat that night was known as The Crescent. It consisted of several outlets which served that part of town and among them was a post office which also served as a newsagent and sweet shop, a grocer, a fruit and vegetable shop, a baker, a butcher, a ladies hairdresser, a dry cleaner and a building society. In most cases, the flats above these shops were let on weekly leases to holidaymakers because they had extensive seaviews to the rear. During the day it was a busy little complex but at night, it looked rather isolated because it stood prominently on a junction with traffic passing by even during the late-night hours. One road led out of town, the other into the centre and the third through a housing estate onto the cliff top.

As I strode towards The Crescent to check all the shops for security, I realized a ladder was standing in front of the building society premises. It reached from the pavement up to the first storey which was a flat, but there was no one with it.

Immediately I thought it might be the burglar we were seeking, but when I shone my torch up to the first-floor windows, all seemed secure with no signs of a break-in. Quickly I checked all the other first-floor windows facing the street, and all the shop fronts, and all were secure. But would a burglar tour the town with a ladder on his shoulder? Even in the darkness of the early hours? A ladder could indeed be classed as a housebreaking implement but at half-past three in the morning it was very likely to attract attention and suspicion, especially from patrolling police officers. I could not imagine any sane burglar carrying one upon his nefarious activities.

Having checked the front of all the premises, I now had the task of checking the rear which was where any break-in was likely to occur. There was access to the rear via a narrow lane which extended behind all the premises; it was just wide enough to accommodate a single vehicle for deliveries, but at night this area was not illuminated. That made the rear of shops and houses more vulnerable than the front, in addition to which there were often fire escapes and outbuildings with low flat roofs, all of which made entry much easier. I now had the choice of trying to walk down that lane without the burglar realizing I was present – if he was breaking-in, this was his most likely point of entry out of sight. The alternative was to flash my torch ahead of me in the hope of catching him in its beam so that I could identify him but of course, that choice meant he would be aware of my presence and could make a dash for freedom, unless he was actually inside one of the flats. Then he might not realize I was about to tap him on the shoulder.

I decided against using my torch. I would move under cover of the early morning darkness and the shadows of the buildings in the hope of catching him red-handed. I crept around the end of The Crescent, my soft-soled boots making no sound and my dark uniform concealing my presence in the shadows. But after passing only two rear entrances, I saw him. A dark shadow standing on the balcony of one of the first-floor flats, and even in the gloom, I could see the window was open and that his hands were ominously close to the catch. I was about to shine my torch and call for him to come down, in the name of the law, when he turned the tables on me.

Suddenly, I was bathed in a pool of brilliant light from his powerful torch, and I could see nothing as it shone down into my eyes.

Then he shouted, 'Ah, the law! Sorry Constable, I thought it was a burglar.'

'Put that light out, I can't see a thing!' I called back.

'Sorry,' and he obeyed immediately.

I blinked a few times as I tried to recover my sight and in the meantime, he swung a leg over the rails of the small balcony and trotted down to ground level via the adjoining fire escape. Then he joined me. I shone my torch so that it illuminated his face without blinding him. He was about twenty-five years old, I estimated, a slender man with blond hair and an infectious smile. He was dressed in a pair of navy blue overalls and wellington boots.

'So who are you? And what are you doing here?'

'I'm the window cleaner,' he said cheerily. 'I work for Sparks.'

'I thought there was just the two of them, man and wife.'

'There was, but they took me on a month or two ago. Their round has expanded, they had trouble getting finished before the shops and offices opened, so they asked me to help out.'

'And your name?'

'Shaw. Bill Shaw,' and he gave an address in Strensford.

'So if you're a window cleaner, where is all your gear?'

'My ladder's out front, I don't need it

round here, not with all these balconies and fire escapes but I do need it for the next job out front. And my leather and bucket are up on that balcony where you saw me, and my cart is at the other end of this lane.'

'Cart?'

'Handcart, with all my gear in it. You can't walk around town carrying all that stuff on your back, especially a ladder. It's behind that garage you can see from here.'

I knew what he meant by his cart. The window cleaners he had mentioned were a husband and wife in their late fifties, their surname being Sparks. That was the legend on their handcart: it said 'Sparks for Sparkle. Professional window cleaners', followed by their address and telephone number. They used handcarts to transport their water, buckets, brushes, leathers, ladders and what-ever they required, sometimes using the ladders to guide the cart.

The ladders, while the cart was moving, were firmly fixed to brackets and functioned as useful handles for steering and pushing. And, of course, a silent hand-propelled cart was unlikely to rouse people from their beds. Sparks started their rounds at 3 a.m., cleaning their customers' shop, office, school, factory or garage windows before they opened for business. They also cleaned glass doors and so, as the people started work, all business premises knew their glassware was scrupulously clean.

Bill Shaw led me to the handcart he was using and sure enough, it belonged to the Sparks' firm for it bore their name and other details. I saw it contained all his equipment, except for the ladder and whatever he had left on the balcony but I took that opportunity to surreptitiously check that it did not contain any stolen goods. I saw none.

'I saw the window was open,' was my next comment, wondering if he could have opened it without breaking the glass. That was sometimes possible. By inserting a thin-bladed knife, a latch could easily be undone on some windows.

'You'd be amazed how many people leave their windows open when they're away,' he said. 'We see them all the time and mostly we try to close them, but that one's swinging open. I was trying to fasten it when you turned up but there's no way I can do it from the outside. Come and have a look.'

Without waiting for my response he led me to the foot of the fire escape and we clambered up. When I stepped onto the balcony, I could see his bucket, wash leather and dry duster with the window standing open like a door.

It had a single catch which could only be operated from the inside and when he pushed on the frame, the window went into the closed position, but immediately swung open an inch or two. The only way to secure it was to lean something against it, and I made a particular check that none of the glass was broken. There was absolutely no evidence he had opened it.

'I'll leave a note in our office,' I told him. 'They'll get a day duty constable to try and contact the keyholder and get it secured.'

'It's a real invitation to a burglar,' he said. 'Just climb up here, step inside and bingo, there's a rich haul to be taken.'

'We've had a spate of burglaries lately,' I told him. 'Flats like this being raided, stuff being taken like radios, cameras, binoculars, things easily passed on without question. Can you keep your eyes open when you're working? Let us know? Description of the burglar, car number, anything in fact.'

'Sure, but I can't see any sensible burglar would risk being seen by folks like us and no sane crook would carry a ladder around with him! And we're always about from the early hours, doing most of the business premises. And you lads are on duty as well.'

We had a long chat and I concluded he was not the burglar, although I did later find Mr and Mrs Sparks in town, working their way along the main street to clean shop and office windows and doors from their familiar handcart. I asked them about Bill Shaw and they confirmed he worked for them, saying he was a reliable and good worker, even if his post was only temporary.

He was not a local man, they added. He said he'd worked in the mining industry in the West Riding. He'd lost his job and had come to Strensford to try and find seasonal employment, and then the window cleaning job had turned up, giving him an income even if it was merely temporary. I mentioned the burglaries and they were aware of them, other officers having briefed them but they could not offer any previous sightings of burglars. And so I continued my patrol until it was time to clock off-duty.

I informed Sergeant Mason of my chat with Bill Shaw and he accepted my opinion that he was not the burglar, chiefly because he had no stolen goods in his handcart, there was no sign of a break-in at the flat where I'd found him. And of course; he was touring the town with a handcart clearly bearing his employer's details. He was not trying to be secretive.

Having booked off-duty at 6 a.m., it was then time to return to Aidensfield. As I motored across the moors with the sun rising and flooding the landscape with its brilliance, a thought suddenly occurred to me, one which had its origins in my knowledge of how magicians and illusionists misdirected their audiences. If a man wanted to be a burglar, what better cover was there than being a window cleaner? Especially with a handcart in which to conceal and carry away his ill-gotten gains. And to carry his ladder. I remembered that a ladder had been used to commit some of those reported burglaries! As Bill Shaw and I had said, what sane burglar would carry a ladder about with him? But if he could transport it around and then climb it without raising suspicion, then he was very sane indeed.

When I got home, I rang the CID at Strensford and explained my theories whereupon they said they would visit Bill Shaw and check his previous history. But when they got to his address, he had left. No one knew where he had gone but after his departure, the burglaries ceased. Nonetheless, a description of him and his alleged activities was circulated, particularly as we discovered his name was not really Bill Shaw.

It was six months later when I learned that a man calling himself Bill Shaw had been arrested for burglary in Bridlington; he was working for a window cleaner at the time and using his employer's ladders. He was questioned about the spate of burglaries in Strensford but steadfastly denied them.

Working in a busy seaside resort was a total change from my peaceful moorland beat at Aidensfield, and I knew the experiences would be beneficial for my future career. As I waited for news of either a transfer from Aidensfield as a means of providing yet more practical experience, or even an announcement of my promotion, I returned to my home on the moors.

As my motorcycle carried me across the heathery heights after my final day's duty in Strensford, I saw, in the far distance, a lorry which had evidently run off the road, probably to avoid hitting a sheep. It was in a ditch and as I grew nearer, I saw it belonged to Claude Jeremiah Greengrass. He was standing nearby, scratching his head because he could find no way of driving it back onto the road. The wheels merely spun uselessly in the soft earth, digging themselves deeper each time he tried.

I eased to a halt beside him.

'Trust you to turn up now!' he grumbled. 'I've been stuck here for two and a half hours with not a soul passing by ... so where have you been? There's never a copper about when you want one! I heard you were sunning yourself at the seaside instead of looking after your customers in Aidensfield...'

'Shut up, Claude! I thought it was time I came back here to see what you're up to, I missed you and your schemes when I was in Strensford. So hop on the back, I'll take you to the garage and you can arrange to be towed out of there.'

'Me cadge a lift on a police motorbike? You must be joking! Folks'll think I'm collaborating with the law!'

'All right, stay here, and I'll call at Bernie's garage to ask him to fetch his breakdown truck out for you. He'll have you out of there in no time.'

'Well, make sure it's the first job you do, Constable. He owes me a favour anyroad. Now don't waste time and don't get sidetracked, I'm supposed to be on my way to an important business meeting.'

'And where would that be, Claude?'

'Never you mind, it's private business!'

'See you, Claude.' I was pleased to be resuming my normal duties with my usual grateful customers, and so I turned my front wheel towards Aidensfield.

The publishers hope that this book has given you enjoyable reading. Large Print Books are especially designed to be as easy to see and hold as possible. If you wish a complete list of our books please ask at your local library or write directly to:

Magna Large Print Books
Magna House, Long Preston,
Skipton, North Yorkshire.
BD23 4ND